THERE ARE WORSE PEOPLE

IRINA ANGELOVA

Cover artwork design copyright © 2025 by Niki Lenhart
nikilen-designs.com

Published by Cupid's Arrow Publishing
cupidsarrowpublishing.com

ISBN 978-1-969655-61-6 (Trade Paperback)

FIRST EDITION

10 9 8 7 6 5 4 3 2 1

THERE ARE WORSE PEOPLE

Prologue

I HEAR THE SOFT CREAK of the door behind me, but I don't move. My back is pressed against the cold stone wall of the little alcove I've found, hidden away from the party and the swirl of embarrassment that comes from the last seven years of questionable life choices. I'm trying to hold it together, trying to keep the tears from spilling over. It's so inconvenient, such terrible timing!

Then I hear Jesse's footsteps, steady and unhurried, as he approaches. He doesn't say anything at first, just lets the silence settle around us like a blanket. I can feel him close now, the warmth of his presence against the cold that's been seeping into my bones.

"Ilaria," he says softly, and there's something in his voice that makes the lump in my throat grow even bigger. I want to ignore him, brush him off with some excuse about needing a moment alone, but the truth is, I don't want to be alone. Not now. Not after that.

I finally look up, meeting his gaze. His eyes are filled with concern, and when he steps closer, I don't flinch away. He's always known how to be close without overwhelming me, how to offer support without smothering me.

"You know you don't have to tolerate any of this," he says, his voice a low rumble that somehow makes the space of the nook feel smaller, safer.

"I know," I whisper, my voice trembling despite my best efforts to keep it steady. "But it's not that simple, Jesse. It's …"

"You don't owe them anything," he continues, his voice soft but firm.

I bite my lip, my vision blurring again. "I know that, but they're—"

"They're nothing," he interrupts, the rare edge in his voice slicing through my thoughts. "They don't get to make you feel like this."

His words break something in me, like a dam I've been holding back, pressing against it with shoulders that suddenly feel small, shaky, and powerless. A tear slips down my cheek, and before I can wipe it away, he's there, his thumb brushing it aside—gentle, almost reverent. It's the smallest of touches, but it undoes me completely. I squeeze my eyes shut, letting the tears fall freely now, feeling the walls close in around me as I start to crumble.

And that's when he pulls me in. Strong arms wrap around my shoulders, pressing me to his chest like he's afraid the flood from the broken dam will pull me under if he lets go. I want to protest, to push him away, to tell him I'm fine, but I can't. I just can't. Instead, I let myself collapse against him, let myself feel the steady rise and fall of his breath, the heartbeat that thuds calmly under my ear. It's grounding, this quiet connection, this wordless understanding that he's here, that he's not going anywhere.

I inhale deeply, catching a hint of his cologne—woodsy and clean—blended with the scent of his skin, which my nervous system has already labeled as "home," "safe," "mine," and "an absolute euphoric pleasure." It settles my racing thoughts, anchoring me to the present, to him. And suddenly, the rest of the world feels far away, like a bad dream I can wake up from.

His hand moves to the back of my head, fingers threading through my hair, soothing and tender.

"If you'd let me handle it my way ..." His voice tightens with a controlled edge that makes me glance up at him quickly. His jaw is clenched, and there's a hard glint in his eyes—protective, almost angry. It's a side of him I've seen before, the side that makes me feel safe but also terrified of what he might do if I let him.

Is he talking about a genius business move or a nasty fistfight? Either way ...

"No," I say, shaking my head, even as a part of me craves what he's offering. "I don't want you to get caught up in this dirt."

His expression doesn't soften. If anything, his eyes grow darker, his grip on me tightening as though he's trying to hold back everything he wants to unleash. "Ilaria, I'm already in this. You know that."

I know he is. I know what he means—he's in it because I am. He can't stay away.

He must see the conflict in my eyes because his grip loosens slightly. "Let me take you home," he says, his voice softening. "We'll grab Milan, and we'll go."

I nod against his chest and stay there, letting myself be held. Just for a moment longer, I allow myself to be small, to be fragile, to let someone else be strong for me.

1

Two weeks ago

I'VE ALWAYS BEEN A FOREIGNER.

When I was teaching English in a Chinese city of fifty thousand people, visitors at the food court would film me eating noodles—every single time I was eating them. Or eating anything at all.

When I worked as a tour guide in India for three tourist seasons in a row, my Indian acquaintances invited me to weddings simply because I had blonde hair and gray eyes.

When I worked as a translator in Malta, local men at a business lunch speculated about my breast size, assuming I didn't understand Maltese. How could they have known that, from my very first day, I was having morning coffee with my landlady and quickly picked up the curse words, numbers, and essential tourist phrases? My linguistically trained brain swiftly absorbed phonemes and discerned patterns in the flow of speech, allowing me to see each new country through the lens of its language.

I was a foreigner when I married a Macedonian after three months of dating and plunged headfirst into traditions completely unfamiliar to me, hoping to learn to swim along the way.

Today, after seven years in Macedonia, I still haven't learned to swim. Though one could say I have—I'm easily spotted in a crowded pool of a hundred people: my swim cap is odd, my technique is off, my breathing unsteady. And I have to wear arm floaties. I remain a foreigner, just as I was before. Neither a local passport, nor owning property in my name, nor my heartfelt love for Balkan cuisine has made me Macedonian.

And now, once again, I messed things up: I put the dessert out too early.

"We don't offer sweets to guests right away," my mother-in-law complained, taking the box of wafer rolls from my hands. "They'll think you're trying to send them home!"

"Wasn't that about coffee?" I tried to recall the set of rules I thought had imprinted on my brain over the past years.

"No coffee, no dessert until the end of the visit!" she reminded me in a sharp whisper.

"Okay, I've got to go," I replied irritably, squeezing past her on my way to the living room, where her cousin's son and his wife sat, having dropped by unannounced. I never got used to such visits, though I'd learned to pretend I didn't mind. I'm not the one who'll have to deal with them anyway.

I apologized, explaining that work was waiting—thankfully, it was a weekday, and I had every reason to use work as an excuse. No one needed to know that my schedule was as flexible as I needed it to be. I'll take that fact with me to the grave.

I grabbed my laptop bag, slipped on my high-heel sandals, and within fifteen minutes, I was exactly where I wanted to be.

"Ilaria!" The waiter at my favorite café, Tuscany, waved at me as soon as I walked in. I liked this Macedonian openness that allowed Petar to greet me loudly, even with other customers around.

"How are you?" I asked as I settled into my usual spot by the window. Though there wasn't really a window—the glass wall had been slid open, turning the entire café into one big summer terrace. That's a pity. I had hoped to escape the July heat in the dry, air-conditioned comfort.

"I ordered some T-shirts for Milan," Petar boasted, flashing a youthful smile. He loved dressing like a teenager, despite being several years older than me. He also apparently intended to help my son cultivate a taste in clothes at five years old.

"You've got to stop spoiling us," I tried to sound stern as I set up my computer on the table and plugged it into the charger.

"I want him to be the trendiest guy in town," he said, showing me the H&M t-shirts that had seemingly been handed over to the delivery service.

"He still won't outdo you," I smirked, silently vowing to be the best aunt to Petar's future kids—if he ever has any. But first, he might want to try dating someone for more than a month.

My laptop hummed softly as I began to work. The café was quiet, with only a few patrons scattered around—mostly fashionable grandpas sipping coffee and puffing on cigarettes, and a couple of moms spending another afternoon of maternity leave, rocking prams and picking at their salads.

I glanced up, noticing Petar sitting down to eat as he often did during this time of day. But today, he wasn't alone. A man sat across from him, someone I had never seen before. He had a strong, imposing figure, with a face that seemed to belong to someone I should recognize but didn't. His dark hair was neatly styled, and his broad shoulders filled the chair as though it had been built for him.

I tried to focus on the document on my screen, my fingers tapping out corrections with mechanical precision. But the low murmur of their conversation reached my ears, making concentration difficult.

"So, how's life in Japan?" Petar's voice carried easily from their table, which was just a meter away. "How are your parents?"

The man responded, his voice a deep rumble. "Japan was ... different. Good, but it's good to be home. My parents are fine; they got a dog."

I forced my attention back to the words on my screen and managed to keep it there for just a few minutes longer.

"No way!" the man exclaimed, his voice tinged with surprise. My fingers froze over the keyboard. What could Petar have told him to elicit such a reaction?

Stefan.

The name slipped into my mind unbidden, and with it came a cold, sticky feeling of dread. My throat tightened, and I forced myself to take a deep breath. *Stop it*, I told myself. There are a thousand things Petar could have told him. The world doesn't revolve around Stefan or my personal drama.

Until I heard Petar say it. "That's his wife."

At that moment, I was a foreigner again—not just in this town, not just in this country, but in my own skin.

Petar didn't even try to make it less awkward. He introduced us with the same exuberance he always had. "Ilaria, this is Jesse. He went to school with Stefan. He just got back from Japan. And Jesse, this is Ilaria."

Jesse's eyes didn't leave mine as he studied me for a moment longer, making me even more self-conscious. Does this blouse make me look more Macedonian or less? Are these pants too tight on my thighs? Does the expression on my face give away the outraged discomfort I'm feeling right now?

Finally, Jesse spoke, his voice soft but steady. "I'm sorry for your loss."

I nodded stiffly, not trusting myself to say anything more. The words had become a tired refrain, a platitude that lost meaning the more I heard it. I turned my attention back to my screen, hoping the conversation would end there.

But then Petar was summoned by another customer, leaving us alone. Jesse took the opportunity to continue, his tone shifting from formal to familiar. "Stefan was a great man. We were close in school. I spent a lot of time at his place."

I clenched my jaw. How many times had I heard this before? How many people had come out of the woodwork, claiming some special connection to Stefan, as if that gave them a right to my grief?

"How's Aunt Vesna?" Jesse asked, his voice almost nostalgic.

I thought back to today's dessert mishap, to the strained interactions with Stefan's mother. "She's fine," I replied, my tone clipped. "Babysitting her grandchildren."

"Right," Jesse said, his expression brightening. "How's Lazar?"

My mind raced. How much should I tell this man, this stranger who had somehow become a part of my life story without my consent? I certainly wouldn't share the mess of my relationship with Stefan's brother, or how my in-laws won't let me sell the property my own husband left me, or how I still have to share the same living space with them, or how they're fucking hypocrites. Or how despite all of this, my son loves them blindly because he's too pure or too young to see what I see. So, I just said, "Lazar's fine, too," my voice devoid of emotion.

I hoped I was making myself clear that I wasn't into small talk. People usually expected me to ask them questions in return. The only problem was, I never cared to. I didn't even really care to answer theirs in the first place, but that seemed like a line of unnecessary rudeness I wasn't willing to cross.

Luckily, Petar returned and asked me what I wanted to have, and I ordered an iced macchiato, hoping the cold drink would help me focus. But when Petar brought it over, I forgot myself, slipping into a tone I only used with people I trusted.

"When are you going to close the sliding wall?" I asked, my voice carrying a hint of irritation. "It's sweltering in here."

Petar, unfazed, grinned at me. "At 2 pm, ma'am, you know the drill!"

I huffed, not because I expected him to change anything, but because I needed to vent, and we usually vented to each other. I was about to make a quip when Jesse suddenly spoke up.

"Can't you close it now?" he asked Petar, his tone firm.

Petar shook his head apologetically. "Manager's orders. At 2 pm, bro."

Jesse frowned, clearly not satisfied. "Your customer is uncomfortable. Don't you guys think you should do something about that?"

I felt a knot of guilt tighten in my stomach. I hadn't meant for this to become an issue. "Really, it's fine," I interjected, trying to diffuse the situation. "I was just teasing him."

But Jesse wasn't letting it go. "You're a regular here, aren't you? You should be able to ask for the AC if you need it."

I blinked, taken aback by his insistence. "I only order a coffee and work here for hours. I don't think that qualifies as being a real customer."

"Do you come here often?" he asked, his eyes locking onto mine with a determination that made my pulse quicken.

Primal resolve flickered beneath the shadow of his dark lashes, like he already knew the answer but wanted me to say it, just so he could follow up with whatever urgent conclusion was poised on the tip of his tongue.

I hesitated, watching Petar move towards the back office. God, I hope he's not really bringing the manager. "Every day," I mumbled.

"Well, that's 2,400 denars a month," Jesse calculated quickly. "Unless they want to lose a regular to the coffee shop across the road, where the AC's on all day, they should take good care of you."

The way he said "*take good care of you*" sent an unexpected shiver down my spine. His voice was so assured, so resolute, that I couldn't help but react. My skin prickled with a mix of irritation and something I didn't want to acknowledge.

"Do they teach this in Japan?" The words slipped out before I could stop them.

Jesse looked startled. "What?"

"To solve other people's problems without them asking first?"

For a moment, we just stared at each other. Jesse's face shifted, confusion mingling with something else. I couldn't tell, and I didn't want to think about it. The guilt was already gnawing at me, making me regret the outburst. Here came the unnecessary rudeness.

"Sorry," I muttered, quickly gathering my things. I didn't look at him again as I packed my laptop and slipped it into my bag. "I have to go."

As I hurried out of the café, it wasn't until I was halfway home that I realized I hadn't paid for my coffee.

•   •   •

A massive car pulled up in front of our house just as I was petting a familiar dog passing by, all while bickering with my brother-in-law.

"Don't get them used to it, or they'll start hanging around here," he grumbled, adjusting the lawn sprinkler. I had felt his disapproving gaze on me for the last five minutes and knew he was going to say something along those lines.

"I'm not feeding him," I replied, continuing to scratch the thick fur of the small mutt with a tag on its ear, indicating it had been vaccinated.

"That doesn't matter; they still get attached."

"Oh, come on, it's just a dog. He's walking on the sidewalk, not even stepping onto your precious lawn."

"Our kids are on that sidewalk all the time!" His voice carried open irritation, giving me the green light for a full-blown response, but I stuck with a little science TED-talk.

"You know," I stood up and turned to face him, "kids who grow up around animals develop more empathy!"

What I didn't say, of course, was that this clearly didn't apply to him—since I knew he had plenty of dogs growing up, right until he got married. Which made me wonder if that scientific fact really held up after all.

Empathy my ass.

When his wife, Danche, had her first baby, he asked Stefan not to cut wood in the yard while the baby was sleeping and told his mom not to talk loudly on the phone outside because she was too loud and would wake the baby.

When my son was born, Lazar was using a wet saw to cut tiles on his terrace—right above our bedroom. When I brought it up to him, he simply said he needed to replace the tiles and couldn't help it.

As I stood there watching him, a flood of memories rushed through my mind—countless little stories proving just how skillfully my in-laws can twist any situation in their favor. Then, I heard the sound of an approaching car.

A gray Kia slowed beside me, giving the dog room to cross the road as soon as I stopped petting him. The car seemed far too large for the narrow local streets. There weren't many of these giants in the city, and I was certain I hadn't seen this one before. My son was obsessed with cars, and everywhere we went, he'd point them out, naming the brands. By now, I was pretty sure I knew all the cars in town.

I was about to head into the house to avoid continuing the pointless argument with Lazar, but I noticed his intrigued gaze fixed on the Kia behind me, and I turned back again. The car parked along the sidewalk opposite our front yard, and my breath caught in my throat when I recognized the driver.

He stepped out, taller than I had thought (since I'd never seen him standing), holding my laptop charger in his hand, and I cursed under my breath.

It seemed Jesse heard me; his brows furrowed slightly, a carefully concealed curiosity in his eyes.

"Jesse!" Lazar suddenly exclaimed, wiping his hands on his shorts as he walked toward my new acquaintance—though, by the looks of it, not so new to him.

"Lazar, how's life?"

Ah, right, Jesse mentioned he'd spent a lot of time in this house. I wonder how many years ago that was? And who was he closer with—Stefan or Lazar? There was only a three-year gap between the brothers, but they never had mutual friends, neither as kids nor as grown-ups.

Lazar was shaking Jesse's hand so vigorously that I felt a chill in my stomach. It seemed like he was in Lazar's camp. Jesse had unwarrantedly defended me at the café and brought me the charger despite my rude behavior, and for a moment, I thought he was on *my* side. But apparently, there would always be more of *them*.

"What brings you here? Have you been in town long?"

"I've been here a week," Jesse replied, stepping closer to hand me the charger. "You left this at the café."

"Thanks," I mumbled, taking the cord from his hand. Lazar smirked.

"Did you come all the way for a charger? She could've picked it up tomorrow."

I closed my eyes and took a deep breath. If Lazar worked on his laptop more often than swung his balls around for fun, he'd know that laptops tend to run out of battery.

I would've realized the charger was missing by evening and had to rush back to the café.

Jesse's voice broke through my thoughts. "I figured your laptop might run out of power, and you wouldn't be able to work."

I opened my eyes and met his gaze, open and kind. Like he was on *my* team after all. Like Lazar's pretentious bullshit couldn't faze him. Like my own outrageous act back at "Tuscany" hadn't been enough, and he was looking to gather more proof that I was every bit the bitch I'd made myself out to be.

"Coffee?" Lazar asked him.

Jesse glanced at me briefly, then checked his watch and agreed.

"Sure, if you're not too busy."

"Of course, we're not busy. Come on!" Lazar led him down the path to our terrace. I hated when he invited himself and his guests onto my terrace. He had his own, right above ours on the second floor, and after that decisive fight between Stefan and his brother, I had made it clear to everyone that the territorial boundaries would be stricter from now on. *No more "ours"; take your shit and head back to your own space! And on your way, try not to brush against my bamboo, you jerk.*

But he knew I wouldn't cause a scene in front of a guest. Besides, even though Lazar had decided to play the host, Jesse had come because of me, and technically, he was *my* guest.

"Ilaria, could you make us some coffee?" Lazar called, pulling out the plastic chairs, and there wasn't even a hint of a question in his tone.

I nodded, biting my lip and swallowing my irritation. Of course, I'll make the damn coffee. I went to the kitchen, gathered the necessary ingredients, and silently noted yet another contradiction in local customs: you're absolutely not supposed to offer guests coffee right away! But today, it's okay because you managed to say the magic words, "come for coffee," which gives you the right to jump straight to the last stage of the visit.

When I returned, they were already seated on the terrace. Lazar was animatedly talking about the city and how it had changed (become emptier for sure). I placed the tray on the table and sat down quietly. Vesna joined us, gushing over how happy she was to see Jesse and how she remembered him and Stefan together when they were fifteen-year-old troublemakers.

So, he was *Stefan's* friend. A weird feeling of unjustified relief spread under my skin.

Jesse answered their questions about where he'd been and how long he planned to stay.

"I need to help my parents with some family matters. The vineyards. They can't work them anymore, so we're going to sell. And I was offered a project here, so I'll be staying for a while."

"Then there's no need to sell, since you're here," Vesna hinted not-so-subtly that he could roll up his sleeves and work in the field.

"If I do sell them, I have some ideas for what to do with the money. Something that would be more beneficial to the city," he caught my intrigued gaze and backpedaled a bit. "But it's just talk for now, so ..."

Lazar nodded approvingly as if Jesse's life decisions had passed some unspoken test.

"That's great. So, you're in construction?"

I kept my eyes on my cup, feeling Jesse's occasional glances. Like he was checking if I was still breathing. I knew why he was looking—I wasn't participating in the conversation. And here I thought we were past that understanding.

At some point, Vesna did what she always did—started bragging about her daughter-in-law, meaning me. Because I was part of her resume.

"Ilaria works with languages. She's traveled a lot, you know, and works as a translator."

I looked up and met Jesse's gaze. There was genuine interest in his eyes, a curiosity that seemed almost too intense in the brown irises.

"What languages do you work with?" he asked.

"Chinese, Macedonian, Hindi, and English," I replied, trying to keep my voice steady.

Something clicked in his mind, reflected in his expression, which became more determined as he asked the next question.

"Do you translate documents?"

"Yes, I have the authority of a notary translator," I said, wondering where this was leading.

"I might need a translator for a project I'm working on. Can I call you about it?"

"Of course," I answered, and under the watchful eyes of Lazar and Vesna, I gave him my number.

The conversation naturally shifted to Stefan. My heart clenched when they started talking about him, about how he died. I no longer felt that violent wrench in my gut, that twisting sensation that turned my stomach inside out, like in the first three months. A year had passed, and I'd grown accustomed to the void in my chest. I'd made peace with it and stopped fearing it. It's just there, and it won't kill me.

Milan dashed out of the house, his little face glowing with excitement. He'd been playing inside, ignoring the conversation, but then he realized something was happening on the terrace without him. I wondered to myself if Jesse would recognize Stefan in him. They were friends as kids, and in all of Stefan's childhood photos, a similar blond, hazel-eyed boy, just like Milan, stared back at me.

"The other car was smashed, too," Lazar continued, while I felt an icy grip tighten around my throat.

"Maybe we shouldn't talk about this right now?" I said, gesturing to Milan.

Lazar looked at me as if I'd said something absurd.

"He understands everything. You dragged him to the funeral, didn't you?"

I shot him a furious look, holding back the reply burning on my tongue. Back then, they had all been very articulate in their protest against me bringing a four-year-old to his father's farewell. But I still did it. He needed to say goodbye, and no, it wasn't too early. It is, however, too early to lose a dad at four, but that I couldn't change, could I?

There was so much I wanted to say to Lazar's smug face, so much I wanted to scream, but I didn't. Not in front of Jesse. Not in front of Milan. Instead, I stood up and took my son's hand.

"Let's go inside. We'll do some drawing, just you and me."

As I walked away, I felt Jesse's gaze on me again, and for a moment, I wanted to believe that he was as angry as I was. But more likely, he saw nothing unusual in this scene, nothing that would make him despise Stefan's family the way I do.

2

STEFAN AND I USED TO VISIT others and host gatherings, though not as often as Lazar and Danche. We quickly realized that these showy get-togethers, whose purpose was just to check a box, were a waste of time and decided to spend it with those we genuinely called friends or, at the very least, whose company we knew we'd enjoy. Given that we lived under the same roof, the contrast was stark: every two weeks, a line of cars would form near our house, bringing guests to their door, while for us, it happened only once every three months.

It didn't bother me because, once we abandoned these unnecessary rituals, it felt like we could finally breathe. I loved that about Stefan—he couldn't stand the hypocrisy either. When you sit at a table with people who are merely friends in name, you inevitably find yourself caught in a race for titles you never signed up for. Who earns more? Did the political party put them up for the job? Why do they go on vacation so often? When are they finally going to put up a fence?

I began devoting my time only to those I loved and who loved me—people who could say anything to my face and ask the most uncomfortable questions without falling apart. People who didn't care why we hadn't put up a fence yet. This drastically reduced my social circle, and it felt like a profound detox. Light and good.

So when another line of cars appeared outside our home, I felt relieved that they weren't here for me. Milan and I were just about to head to the racetrack. As I waited for him on the terrace, every guest who climbed the stairs to the second floor greeted me with a judgmental smile.

"Hello, Ilaria," they'd say, while their faces screamed, *There goes that crazy woman who doesn't even attend her sister-in-law's birthday.*

You bet I don't attend. I'd rather lick a toilet seat and build that damn fence brick by brick than listen to your strained attempts at playing virtuous members of society—boasting about distant relatives who made it in Germany while condemning divorced women and those who dare do their laundry outside of the cheap electricity hours.

That socially acceptable form of misogyny was giving me whiplash.

So was the fact that Danche had been kind to me during my first years in this house—until I found out she'd been telling everyone behind my back that I came here already pregnant, all while smiling and saying 'good morning' to my face. Apparently, we had announced my pregnancy unfathomably soon. Because obviously, no one gets fertilized on the first try.

Family, right?

And sisterhood. Girl power.

So fucking confusing.

As guests arrived en masse for the party, Milan came running out of the house, announcing that he was heading upstairs with the others—followed by my mother-in-law, who had apparently dressed him and convinced him that a grown-up's birthday party was more fun than a trip to the racetrack. I wanted to strangle her for making decisions about my child without me, but Milan looked so excited that I remembered why I'd been tolerating them all.

My curses went unsaid as I watched the two of them walk away with a dark gaze, just as an unknown number flashed on my phone's screen.

"Hello, Ilaria?" The voice was familiar, deep and smooth, flashing the brown irises in my memory.

"Yes ..." I hesitated, my mind scrambling to place him.

"It's Jesse. We met recently at the café."

I breathed a little easier. "Yes, I remember. Hi."

"I'm calling about some work. You mentioned you do translations?"

"I did."

"I have a set of documents that need notarized translations into English."

"How many pages?"

"Twelve."

I evaluated the workload. "They'll be ready by Friday."

"Perfect! I can drop the documents off right now. Are you home?"

I paused, looking around at the line of cars in front of the house. "I'm home, but ... could we meet somewhere else?"

A brief pause on his end, then, "Sure ..."

"Let's meet downtown; I can be there in half an hour."

We met at a new Turkish café on the rooftop of a two-story building. Jesse handed me a yellow folder as we met at the bar counter. He was dressed casually but with a certain effortless style that was hard to miss—dark jeans that fit him just right, a charcoal gray T-shirt that hinted at the muscular frame beneath. His hair, a thick mop of dark waves, was neatly styled, but there was a relaxed, almost rugged edge to him that kept him from looking too polished.

"Everything's in here," he said, his voice steady, his presence quietly commanding. Then he looked around and asked, "Do you have time, or are you in a hurry?"

I hesitated, my eyes flicking to a free table next to me, then back to him. Milan was at the party, nobody was waiting for me at home, so I said, "To be honest, this is when I drink my evening coffee."

"Then let's have coffee."

As we waited for the waiter, I took in the café's ambiance—the soft, golden light that bathed the space in a warm glow, the rich scent of spices mingling with the faint hint of shisha smoke in the air. Around us, the low hum of conversations mixed with the soft clatter of cups and plates.

Jesse leaned back in his chair, his tanned hands on the armrests. "Why didn't you want to meet at home?"

"Lazar has a whole crowd over," I replied, shifting slightly in my seat.

"And?"

I looked away, "I don't like giving people more reasons to talk."

He chuckled softly. "You think me dropping off some documents would be a reason for gossip?"

"Your car alone is reason enough," I said with a smirk, remembering the sleek, expensive machine he drove.

Jesse laughed, a deep, resonant sound that seemed to vibrate through the air.

I went on, "They'd say, '*He definitely didn't bring this car from Japan. I mean, Japan is way too far away. He must have bought it here. Why would he buy it here? Isn't he staying for like a week?*' I'm telling you, there will be some serious brainstorming!"

"I don't mind that," Jesse said as his laughter died out. "People talk, I'm aware of that. It's not exclusive to Macedonia, you know."

He was right. That's pretty common in small towns though—like the one we lived in.

I found myself remembering the last time he'd come to my house, the way things had unraveled.

"Sorry about the scene at my place the other day," I said, wincing apologetically.

"It's nothing," he replied, waving it off like it was no big deal. "If I lived with my family, I'd be arguing with them constantly. I can barely last a week in my parents' house."

"Is that why you've been living in Japan?"

"The last two years, yeah. Before that, it was Dubai, Germany, Turkey ..."

"You really don't like being home, do you?"

"You're far from home too," he said, a challenge in his voice. And in his eyes.

"Yeah ... I've worked in a lot of places."

"China?"

"China, South Korea, Malta, India."

"Wow. And you ended up here, in a town with fifteen thousand people."

"Well, you know, love, marriage, and all that." The words came out more bitterly than I intended, and I looked down, feeling the familiar ache rise in my chest.

Jesse nodded, his gaze softening as if he understood without needing to ask.

"It's good you have help with your son," he said quietly.

"Yeah. It's the only reason I'm still in that house. That, and the fact that my mother-in-law makes phenomenal sarma," I replied, managing a small smile.

Jesse grinned, nodding knowingly.

"Why didn't Stefan get you out of there?" His question was gentle but direct, the kind that cut through the noise and went straight to the heart of things.

I startled and looked up at him; there was no judgment, no prying. Just a quiet concern.

"He wanted to, but ... there are a lot of unresolved issues with the property. When his father died, both brothers and their mother inherited it, and now they can't decide what to do with it. Or rather, they don't want to sell any of it, and without that money, we couldn't build or buy anything. You know how people think here: as long as we have a place to live, there's no need to sell the family property. And now that I've inherited Stefan's share, I can't get them to agree on anything either because, apparently, they enjoy my company. Which is highly doubtful since I don't even hide how much they all hack me off."

I realized I'd said too much and flushed, feeling the heat creep up my neck. But Jesse just smiled, his eyes twinkling with amusement.

"No, no, keep going," he said, laughing lightly. "I can tell you want to."

Just then, the waiter arrived with our coffee, and I felt a sudden lightness, a realization that maybe I could enjoy this moment.

"You know what," I said, brightening up, "if we're going to be venting, I need rakia."

Jesse's grin widened, and he called the waiter back, ordering us drinks. There was something in the way he did it, a casualness that put me at ease.

However, after that, I didn't go on ranting about my family. The conversation drifted to lighter topics: we started swapping stories about our travels, the quirks of other cultures, the strange foods we'd tried, and the people we'd met along the way. I said that the job of a tour guide was the best job I've ever had; he said that during his trips he'd learned the hard way never to trust a local's definition of 'not too spicy.' I found myself laughing more than I had in months.

And then, as it happens in a small town where everyone knows each other, we had a "hi-sayer": a man in his forties approached our table, his presence unsettling. He was neat, well-dressed, with a friendly enough demeanor, but there was something about him that always made my skin crawl.

"Ilaria!" he greeted, his voice too loud, too cheerful.

"Vlatko," I replied, my tone neutral as I glanced at Jesse, who was watching the exchange with quiet interest.

Vlatko's eyes flicked to Jesse, suspicion evident in the way his gaze lingered. They exchanged a brief nod of acknowledgment before Vlatko turned back to me, his smile widening.

"How are you? How's Milan?" he asked, his tone laced with a false concern that made my stomach turn.

"He's fine," I replied shortly, not wanting to engage in small talk. "How's everything with you?"

Vlatko nodded, his eyes still darting between me and Jesse. "I'm here with some friends," he added, as if that explained his interruption. "Just wanted to say hello."

When he finally ran out of his stock phrases made to torture the people he accidentally meets in public and excused himself, heading back to his table, I let out a long sigh and dropped my head onto the table.

"That's why I hate this place," I muttered.

"You hate this place?" Jesse asked, like he wasn't sure he'd heard me right. "The café or the town?"

"The town. I mean, I don't hate it," I said, lifting my head and looking at him. "I love it, a lot. I love the weather, the low crime rate, the food. God, I love the food so much!"

He growled a laugh.

"But sometimes it feels like I don't belong here at all. Or maybe I feel that way too often. But it can't be the place—it's not them, it's me. It has to be me. I mean, so many people can't be wrong."

I noticed the way his jaw tightened slightly, like he was holding back from saying something he really wanted to say. But he hid it behind the amusement in his voice. "You probably shouldn't drink on an empty stomach," Jesse said as he called the waiter over again to order food.

We exchanged a childish glance when the waiter looked at us with frustration, his eyes clearly saying, *"What the fuck is wrong with you two?! Can't you fucking decide so I don't have to come back again?"*

But he couldn't say anything, not in Jesse's presence. Jesse had this strong effect on people, like he was constantly in the middle of the business deal of the century.

"What was it you were trying to say earlier?" he asked as the poor waiter left.

"That guy will tell everyone he saw me with you."

"The waiter?"

"The other guy."

"Oh, that one. And?"

"And the funny thing is, six months ago, he came onto me. And that's okay, right? A guy likes a girl, calls her on a date. Wrong! He's a police officer, by the way—and I personally think that's an important fact in this story for so many reasons. He's a man holding a certain power. And the way he did it was ... He called me to his office, and I thought something important had come up about my status because Stefan had recently died. But he just bluntly offered to have a shag. I almost kneed him in his nuts; I really wanted to. I swear to God, this man had been doing business with Stefan. How fucked up is that? Like, if my husband is dead, I'm automatically available for blunt shag offers? But now he'll spread the word that I've been having drinks with random men. He finally fucking caught me doing what he's been accusing me of in that perverted brain of his. And that's why I hate this place. He just came to say hi, like we're friends. God, I hate this bullshit."

As I stopped talking and pulled my head out of my ass, I noticed the tension in Jesse's face—the way his eyes were narrowing as if he was holding back something—anger, perhaps, or maybe frustration. I bit my tongue immediately. Why did I say all of that? *I really shouldn't be drinking right now.*

"Does this happen often?" he asked, his voice steady but with an edge, a hardness that hadn't been there before.

"You mean, do I often have drinks with random men? Because I don't—"

"Ilaria," he said my name like he owned it, then went on very slowly, as if to make himself perfectly clear, "you can have drinks with anybody you want without having to explain yourself."

I felt my ears burn and smiled sheepishly. "You know it's not like that here."

It used to be like that for me, I think. I came to this country with an opinion and a strong sense of freedom. Does that mean I managed to blend in after all? And my personal values, which had been my compass during all my journeys through different cultures, got dissolved in the nuances of "When in Rome"?

"It can be like that if you make it like that," Jesse says, his tone firm. "But what I was asking was, do you often have to deal with assholes like him?"

Before I could answer, the waiter approached us with an apologetic smile, gesturing toward our table. "Excuse me, but could you move to another spot? We have a large group coming in, and we need to join this table with another one. We'll find you a quieter corner," he offered.

"Sure, no problem," Jesse replied, his tone easygoing. I nodded in agreement—the poor waiter deserved some compliance from our side.

As the waiters began to move our food, a traffic jam of bodies formed, all bustling to accommodate the sudden change. As I tried to step back to make room, the waiter suddenly bumped into me, causing me to stumble awkwardly. Just as I braced for a clumsy fall, I felt strong hands grip my hips firmly.

For a second, my back pressed against a solid chest. I could feel its steady rise and fall against my shoulder blades. The hands lingered on my hips just long enough for me to notice the warmth seeping through the thin fabric of my palazzo pants. A mild woodsy scent rushed into my nose. My heart leaped into my throat, but before I could even register the sensation, Jesse stepped back, releasing me as soon as I found my balance.

"Sorry," I mumbled, the word coming out more breathless than I intended, my face already starting to flush. Jesse was quick to respond.

"No, totally my fault."

He was already two steps away, but I still felt the woodsy scent on the roof of my mouth.

Just as we began to move toward our new table, I caught Vlatko's gaze fixed on us, his eyes narrowing slightly before shifting back to his drink. Jesse noticed too, a slight tension tightening his jaw.

As we settled into the more secluded corner, Jesse gave the space a once-over and said, "Well, this is for the best, I think. At least you won't feel so exposed here."

I glanced around, noting the privacy. It was quieter, yes, but his words carried a different weight, a subtle implication I wasn't sure how to unpack. Before I could say anything, he continued, his tone thoughtful. "I guess you can't do much about people talking or assuming; that's their prerogative. But as for that jerk … maybe you should appear with men in public more often."

I blinked, turning my head to look at him directly. "What?"

Jesse met my gaze with a steady calmness, but there was something behind his eyes—a quiet intensity. "It's good for people like him to know that you're never alone. Maybe he wouldn't dare to stare like that or even approach you after the dick moves he pulled."

I wanted to laugh it off, but the sincerity in his voice kept me from doing so. "Well, I am with someone right now, but it didn't stop him."

"If I was sure you didn't mind me stepping in, I would make him understand," he replied without missing a beat, his eyes not leaving mine.

I felt heat rise to my cheeks again, and I fought the immediate, irrational thought that flickered in my mind. He didn't mean what I thought. He just couldn't. But his gaze remained unwavering, as if waiting for me to respond.

"But from the episode in the coffee shop a couple of days ago, I figured you don't like to be taken care of," he added, his voice dropping just slightly, as if he was treading carefully around the memory.

I cringed internally, remembering how I had brushed him off so coldly. "Right. Sorry about that. I was being a massive bitch. You were being nice."

Jesse nodded, a small, almost playful smile curling his lips. "I was."

I raised an eyebrow at him. "No comments about me being a massive bitch?"

"I don't have a death wish," he shot back, deadpan, and I couldn't help it—I burst out laughing.

"Smart man," I managed between giggles, the tension between us breaking like a wave on the shore.

Jesse leaned back in his chair, a sly grin on his face. "You know," he said, "we've met before."

I blinked, caught off guard. "We have?"

He nodded, a small smile playing on his lips. "At Marjan's wedding, a few years ago. I was there, and I remember catching up with Stefan."

The mention of the times when Stefan was still around made my bones melt in a way both hurtful and warming.

"You were wearing a lemon-colored dress," he continued, his eyes taking on a distant, nostalgic quality. "I remember watching you play with Milan. He was tiny then, maybe two or three. You danced Oro, holding his little hand."

The breath caught in my throat. The image he painted was so vivid, so specific, that it overwhelmed me. That dress was still hanging in my wardrobe—one of those you buy for a certain occasion. I never wore it again.

I opened my mouth to say something, anything, but just then, Jesse's phone rang, cutting through the moment.

He glanced at the screen, his brows furrowing slightly before he apologized to me and answered. "Hello? Oh, Lazar, what's up?"

From Jesse's quiet responses—mostly nods and the occasional "mhmm"—it was clear Lazar was the one doing all the talking. I took a sip of my rakia, the burn seeping through my throat, but my mind kept circling back to what Jesse had just said.

As I cut into a piece of fried cheese from the appetizer board, the golden crust gave way to soft, melted perfection. The warmth of it hugged my tongue, soothing the burn of the rakia, and a soft moan of satisfaction slipped out before I could stop it. My eyes fluttered shut for just a second, savoring the taste. When I opened them, I caught Jesse watching me, his lips lifted into a small, crooked smile.

Suddenly self-conscious, I froze. Did I have crumbs on my face? Did I just roll my eyes like a lunatic? God, I'm never going to eat in public places again!

But his expression wasn't mocking. There was a quiet curiosity in his gaze, like he was seeing something in me for the first time. His eyes stayed on me, unwavering as I chewed, making me hyper-aware of every movement. I grabbed a tissue, wiping my mouth even though I wasn't sure there were crumbs. Crumpling the tissue in my hand, I instinctively licked my lips—just a quick brush of my tongue—and that's when it happened. His gaze, steady until now, finally flicked away, a faint pink rising on his jaw.

After a few minutes, Jesse ended the call with a promise to "see what he could do" and put his phone away with a sigh.

"That was your brother-in-law," he explained. "Apparently, he heard from someone at his party which company I'm working with now, and he wants me to try and get him a contract."

I couldn't help but roll my eyes. "Of course he does. I'm sorry, my family is a huge leech."

Jesse shrugged. "It's okay, that's how most things are solved here. It's not unusual."

"I know," I said, a bit more exasperatedly than I intended. "Please ignore my whining. I'm just negative like that."

He snickered, creases forming in the corners of his eyes. "As every massive bitch should be."

I gave him a mock glower, but quickly softened. "I'll never hate you for telling the truth."

"Truth is subjective," he countered, his gaze locking onto mine, as if testing my logic and judgment.

Without missing a beat, I rephrased, "I'll never hate you for telling *your* truth."

His parted lips stretched into a faint half-surprised, half-sly smile, like he'd just discovered a loophole in the income tax declaration regulations.

"I should be going," I said, glancing down at my phone, more as an excuse than anything else.

Jesse straightened in his chair, the lightness in his expression replaced by something more serious. "Did you drive here?"

I shook my head. "I don't drive."

"Why not?"

I hesitated, searching for the right words. "I don't know … This town is tiny; I can walk anywhere. Besides, I always had someone to drive me—my dad when I lived at home, then a driver assigned by my company. In India, I always had a driver on tours, and later, Stefan drove me whenever I needed. I never really had a reason to learn."

"So, you do like being taken care of, after all."

Jesse's gaze remained fixed on my face, like I'm a jigsaw puzzle he's come really close to solving.

"I guess I do," I said, having no idea where it came from, like this confession was summoned by him from the depth of my subconscious.

"In that case, I'll drive you home."

I shook my head, already picturing the scene it would cause. "Thanks, but no. There are too many people at the house right now. I don't want to give them a show—getting a ride from a man."

He smirked, a playful glint returning to his eyes. "I told you, you should appear in public with men more often."

I rolled my eyes. "I know you like people drooling over your car, but I'll just take a taxi. Besides, haven't you been drinking?"

That's when I noticed his rakia glass was still full and untouched.

"I didn't drink," he said, clearly amused by my surprise.

"Why not?" I nearly exclaimed, feeling foolish for not noticing earlier. How caught up in our conversation had I been?

Jesse leaned forward as if about to share a secret. I instinctively leaned closer, eager to hear whatever he had to say.

"I knew you would let me drive you."

And I did.

He dropped me off in front of the house, where a few pairs of curious eyes watched from the upper terrace. I could feel their stares, and in my gut, I knew this was what would spark the drama that unfolded the next day.

"YOU'D BETTER LET ME WORK, or I might just have to sell your toy car collection," I warned Milan, waving him off toward the small play area by the café. My voice carried just the right blend of threat and humor, though inside, I was already envisioning the cozy little villa those toy cars could buy.

Milan's protest was immediate and indignant, but predictably short-lived. He vanished into the plastic maze, though I knew he'd be back, like a boomerang that never failed to return.

With a deep breath, I tried to refocus on the open document glowing on my laptop screen, but my concentration scattered. Tuscany was quiet—almost too quiet, save for the soft hum of conversation at a couple of occupied tables and the low strains of music that I hoped would cover the conversation I was about to have.

I pulled out my phone and dialed Jesse, steeling myself for the inevitable.

"Done with the translation already?" His voice caught me off guard, casual and too confident.

"Translation?" I stuttered, momentarily thrown. I hadn't even started, and his assumption knocked the words I'd been carefully lining up in my head right off the shelf. I scrambled to regroup, but the irritation seeped into my voice.

"No, I'm working on it right now." And then I said it. "Listen, I need you to be straight with me. Did anything I said yesterday make you think I was advising you against working with Lazar?"

"What? No ..." He sounded baffled, like I'd just asked him if the grass was blue. There was the distant sound of children shouting, and I wondered if he was outside. "Why?"

"Are you sure? Because I've been racking my brain, and maybe I said something about leeches, but that wasn't about Lazar's professionalism. He's one of the best in town."

"What's going on?" Jesse's voice dropped, growing serious, and I was a bit nervous at its sound, but I made myself power through it.

"You turned him down, didn't you?"

"How do you know that?"

"Because he thinks I turned you against him."

"He told you that?"

"Yes. He saw you drop me off, and now he's convinced I talked you out of signing with him."

Jesse clicked his tongue, annoyance creeping in. "I turned him down because we already have a supplier under contract. It has nothing to do with you," he snapped, his tone sharp, before muttering a soft curse. "Hold on, I'll call you back."

"No, wait—" I shouted, but I knew it was too late. Jesse was going to call Lazar, and that would only pour gasoline on the fire Lazar had already kindled. The line went dead, and now it was my turn to curse.

Five minutes ticked by, then ten, and still no call back. I already imagined myself moving out of the house—not because I'd finally decided to and found a nice rental place, but because I couldn't stand the awkwardness and guilt that stung. It wasn't that I cared about Lazar's career, but knowing that I'd be held responsible for missed opportunities every time we met in that house, in that yard, on the way to the outdoor trash can sounded too intense to stick around voluntarily.

Milan reappeared periodically, thrusting bugs and spiders into my line of sight, each one a new distraction that I couldn't help but entertain. The text on my laptop glared at me accusingly, and I stared back at it, silently apologizing for my divided attention.

And then, just as my patience was fraying, the door swung open, and there they were—Jesse, and a little girl just a tad younger than Milan.

The girl spotted the play area immediately and bolted, while Jesse strode over to my table, looking as if he'd run a marathon.

"No one warned me that playgrounds are a whole different kind of sport," he said, dropping into the seat across from me, slightly winded.

"I wouldn't know. I avoid them like the plague."

"You don't take Milan to playgrounds? How do you pull that off?"

"I go where I need to go, and Milan tags along. He's got to find his own entertainment, which I think is good for creativity. Sometimes he lucks out, and there's a plastic slide in the vicinity."

Jesse glanced over at the two little gremlins now negotiating the seesaw.

"And she's … ?" I nodded toward the blonde girl in the blue dress.

"My niece. My sister just had her second baby two months ago, and she's drowning a bit, so I take Bisera out when I can."

I raised an eyebrow, impressed by his dedication, though my smile felt tight. Jesse noticed and leaned in, his expression softening.

"Look, I'm sorry about the misunderstanding. I thought I was clear with Lazar."

"Please tell me you didn't just call him."

"Of course I did."

I groaned, feeling the weight of the situation settle over me. "Great. Now he's going to think I complained to you."

"What exactly did he say?"

"It doesn't matter. You know what? Let's just drop it." I waved a hand, trying to shake off the frustration. "Sorry, I'm a bit on edge today. My mother-in-law is watching Danche's kids, and usually, she takes Milan upstairs to play while I work. But today, Danche wouldn't let Milan up because he had a cough three days ago. I would've pointed out that her kids are always sick when they come over, but I didn't get the chance because Lazar barged in with his complaints ..."

"I'm really sorry you're having trouble because of me," he said, searching my face for any signs of anger I might want to spill on him, like he was ready to take it. But I didn't have any. Not towards him.

"It's not your fault," I sighed, and added more to myself than to him. "I just need to get out of that place."

"I won't argue with that."

Milan returned, proudly displaying yet another bug, and I couldn't help but sigh even louder. It was the tenth one.

"Sweetheart, why don't you go play with that cool girl while Mommy works?" I said in an almost whining voice.

Jesse caught a glimpse of my laptop screen and stood up, offering me a reassuring smile. "I'll keep them busy." He started quizzing Milan about the bug's legs, herding him back to the play area.

Jesse felt guilty. Dealing with people like Lazar was a constant game of second-guessing yourself: Was he being passive-aggressive, or was I overthinking this? Did he twist the situation, or did I really screw up? On the way to the café, I had kept replaying my conversation with Jesse, searching for any hint of a misstep. And now Jesse was doing the same, questioning his own actions, wondering if he'd inadvertently caused the mess.

You couldn't win with people like that. Sometimes it was better not to fight at all.

I turned my attention back to the documents from Jesse's company—a deal involving an investment in a new construction project in Skopje—though I couldn't help but glance up occasionally at the kids. Jesse was fully engaged, sliding them down the slide, examining spider webs with exaggerated interest, mediating their minor squabbles, and teaching them to play *eenie-meenie-minie-moe*. Then Petar joined him, and since there were no customers, they chatted for half an hour while simultaneously supervising the two wild monkeys.

When Jesse and Petar eventually approached me, clearly plotting something, I narrowed my eyes, bracing for whatever they were about to drop on me.

Jesse spoke first, his tone casual but his words precise. "Igor Dzhambazov's performing at the square Friday night. Petar's going."

"Yes," Petar chimed in, "and a couple of girls from the bar. You know them."

"I'm pretty sure your relatives won't be there, though I can't guarantee it. Want to come?" Jesse's voice was casual, but there was an undercurrent of hesitation, as if he was testing the waters, unsure of what he might stir up. His eyes lingered on mine, searching for a reaction.

I raised an eyebrow, a teasing smile tugging at the corner of my lips. "How long did you practice that pitch?"

He deadpanned, but there was humor in his eyes. "Did it work?"

"Maybe."

"It starts at eight-thirty. I'll pick you up." He leaned in just a fraction, his gaze steady.

I quickly glanced at Petar again, and he nodded at me in amusement. I half-hated, half-loved the way they ganged up on me, and somehow I knew that hanging out with them could be good, so I gave in, "I have to put Milan to bed. I'll meet you at the square at nine."

"Deal." Jesse straightened up, and his usual playful demeanor returned. "Now, if you'll excuse me, I'm taking these two meerkats to the fair."

"Seriously?"

"Yep." His grin was wide, almost boyish, as he started to herd the kids toward the door. "Don't worry, I'll feed them and buy them a bunch of junk. Milan won't even remember you exist for the next couple of hours."

"Thanks," I called after him, watching Milan hop excitedly toward the exit, his little feet barely able to contain his enthusiasm. The promise of "buying a bunch of junk" had clearly worked its magic.

As they disappeared through the door, I pressed my lips together, a strange mix of relief and nervousness settling in. Turning to Petar, who had dropped himself into his usual spot at the table, I asked, "I can trust him with my kid, right? You better tell me the truth or find somebody else to buy Zara T-shirts for."

Petar chortled as he prepared to bite into his club sandwich. Then he looked at me, and I knew he meant it when he said, "He's the most reliable guy I know."

•　　　•　　　•

The taxi wound its way through the quiet streets, with Milan pressed against the window, eagerly scanning the passing houses. My phone buzzed in my lap with Jesse's message, a follow-up to our earlier conversation when I called to tell him the translation was ready. He'd offered to pick it up, as usual, but today, I insisted on dropping it off. "I'm heading downtown with Milan," I'd said. "I can drop it off wherever you need."

There was a short pause on the line before he responded, "I'm home, actually. Why don't you bring it over?"

I hesitated, briefly weighing the idea. "Sure. Just send me the address."

And now here we were, the taxi winding through a neighborhood I hadn't visited in years. The houses were modest but well-kept, with small gardens in full bloom. The taxi slowed as we reached a wrought-iron gate, and there, standing by the entrance, was Jesse. He raised a hand in greeting, a smile tugging at the corners of his lips.

"Come on in," he called out. "It's coffee time."

"We're actually on our way downtown for pancakes," I protested, catching the scent of something sweet and warm wafting from an open window.

Jesse's grin widened. "Perfect timing, then. I'm making pancakes. My sister is here with Bisera. You should join us."

Before I could object, Milan spotted Bisera—the little girl from the café—running out of the house. She waved at him, and without a second thought, he dashed after her, disappearing into the yard.

"Looks like we're staying," I muttered, more to myself than to Jesse as I paid the driver. Jesse only chuckled, holding the gate open for me as I followed him inside.

The house was a modest two-story structure, its facade plain except for a few stray vines creeping up the walls. The yard, though spacious, was untouched—no flowers, just an expanse of grass that looked like it had been mowed only occasionally. It had the unmistakable look of a place lived in by someone who wasn't around much, who had built it years ago and left without having a chance to call it home.

Jesse led me to the dining room, where his sister was setting up a small table. Bisera's laughter echoed from the yard, followed by Milan's excited chatter. She looked up and smiled warmly at me, waving me over.

"So, this must be the famous Milan my daughter wouldn't shut up about," she said, pointing at the kids through the window. "I'm Betty, Jesse's sister."

Betty was a dark-haired woman in her late twenties, a softer, shorter version of Jesse. Her eyes were kind, and she had the same easygoing demeanor as her brother.

"Nice to meet you," I said, shaking her hand. "I'm Ilaria."

She nodded knowingly and gave her brother, who was flipping a pancake in the adjoining kitchen like a master chef, a quick, conspiratorial look. "Would you like coffee with your pancakes?" she asked, pulling out a chair for me.

I appreciated the offer. Regardless of traditions, I was someone who always asked for coffee as soon as I entered someone's house. If I had to focus on a long conversation, I needed caffeine to power me through it.

"Sure," I said, but before I could sit down, Bisera's voice came from outside, summoning her mom. "Go ahead, I'll handle the coffee."

"Don't worry, just sit—Jesse will take care of it," Betty threw back as she disappeared through the back door.

"I really want to help," I told Jesse, approaching the kitchen. I hoped he wouldn't insist on me sitting down and waiting for him to do all the work, though I knew guests weren't usually expected to barge into the kitchen. It was considered more of a utility area, an ugly, messy workspace, as opposed to the neat and shiny dining room that showcased the hosts' best intentions toward their guests.

But here was a man making breakfast, handling the ladle like it belonged in his big, muscular hand, which was quite a rare occurrence in the Balkans (not the muscular hand, but the ladle in it). So, I found inexplicable confidence within me that he wouldn't wave my offer off. And he didn't.

"Go ahead," he said, showing me the shelf where the coffee and blender were stored. "Make yourself at home. It's not one of those houses where we refuse help." He grinned.

"I'm glad it isn't."

"Besides, I'd rather you make the coffee. It was really good last time at your place."

I got the glasses from the shelf. "It's next to impossible to mess up cold coffee."

"You wouldn't believe it. My sister's an expert in that. She whips it up to the brim, leaving very little space for milk."

"You gotta love a thrifty woman," I grinned.

"Yeah, well, if I wanted black coffee, I'd go for Turkish," he said, dropping the last pancake on top of the ruddy pile and taking it to the dining room.

As I got the sugar from the shelf and opened the Nescafe can, I turned around to search for a spoon and bumped right into his chest, instinctively throwing my hands forward. Apparently, he'd come back for something, but I hadn't heard or anticipated his quick return. I took a step back, but there was nowhere to go. My back was against the counter, and Jesse was right there, his body warm and solid in front of me.

"Oh!" I exclaimed, startled.

"Sorry," Jesse said quickly, his hands raised to my sides but never landing on me, as if he wasn't sure what the right move was.

He was close—so close that I could see the faint shadow of stubble along his jawline, smell the faint cedarwood scent that I realized I had memorized over the few times we'd spent together. I looked up, meeting his gaze. His eyes, a deep, steady brown, were focused on my face until they flicked down, just briefly, to where the neckline of my summer dress dipped slightly, revealing a bit of cleavage. It was a simple dress, light blue and sleeveless, flowing just above my knees. The fabric clung softly to my skin, and I suddenly became acutely aware of how it might appear to him.

"I was just trying to find the spoons," I murmured.

Jesse's gaze snapped back to my eyes, and a faint, almost guilty smile lifted his full lips. "Didn't mean to trap you here," he said, his voice lower than before.

I swallowed, trying to steady my breathing. "It's okay," I managed to say. "I'm sure that's just part of your hosting program, and all your guests get trapped in the kitchen eventually."

He chuckled, a low, rumbly sound. "Not all of them." He took a small step back, giving me just enough space to slip past him. "Spoons are over there."

Just then, the kids burst into the kitchen, bringing with them a whirlwind of energy. Milan and Bisera, faces alight with excitement, immediately zeroed in on the plate of pancakes on the dining table. Betty swooped in to guide them toward the sink, reminding them to wash their hands first. I used the moment to take a breath.

I guess I don't need caffeine anymore.

I found the spoons and got back to work, blending the coffee powder with water until it frothed up just right, and added cold milk and ice cubes. I handed one glass to Jesse, who accepted it with a quick nod of thanks. He took a sip and then raised an eyebrow, clearly impressed.

"I'm telling you, you've got the magic touch," he said, gesturing with his glass before setting it down. "I might have to recruit you as my personal barista."

I smirked. "As long as you keep flipping those pancakes."

He chuckled, and we started setting the table together, passing plates, forks, and napkins in an unspoken rhythm. The kids, now clean-handed, darted back to the table, eyeing the pancakes like they were treasure.

Jesse handed Milan a small jug of milk, and Bisera grabbed the chocolate spread before anyone else could.

"So," I started, glancing at Jesse with a teasing smile, "what's with the name Jesse, anyway? It doesn't exactly scream 'Macedonian.'"

Jesse grinned, clearly amused by the question. "It's Alexander. Jesse is a nickname. Do you know Jesse James?"

I frowned, shaking my head. "No, I don't think so."

Alexander suited him.

"He was a Wild West train robber. They made a lot of movies about him. My friends started calling me that at some point, and it stuck."

I took a bite of my pancake, and out of the corner of my eye, I saw Jesse's mouth part slightly as he watched me. It was like déjà vu—reminiscent of that Turkish café, his gaze locking onto me with the same intensity, his pupils dark and dilated. But this time, it felt even more charged, more deliberate. The fucked-up part was, it didn't feel intrusive. It felt ... right. Like all my past breakfasts, lunches, and dinners had gone tragically unnoticed, and now I couldn't imagine eating without him watching me.

I swallowed, feeling his gaze trace the movement of my throat. "Were you into those movies?" I asked, casually taking a sip of coffee.

"No," he said, his voice a little rougher, his eyes following the line of my neck. "I was into the ugly stage of my puberty."

I laughed, and Betty chimed in, "Oh, he was terrible growing up."

Jesse shot his sister a playful glare. "What do you know? You were like eight when I was fifteen."

"Mom likes talking about it," she quipped back.

"That doesn't count," Jesse retorted, waving a hand dismissively. "You should find some real witnesses."

Betty grinned wickedly. "I'm sure they're all dead."

The words hung in the air for a split second too long. The playful atmosphere dipped slightly as the unintended weight of Betty's comment settled. Jesse was the first to react, his expression shifting as he hissed, "Jesus, Betty."

I doubted she had known Stefan personally, I wouldn't expect a little girl to know all her fifteen-year-old brother's friends. It's just the news in this fun-size town spread impressively fast when someone was born or turned up dead. Especially in a grisly car crash. *That* had made fucking news on the national television a year ago.

Betty's face fell, realization dawning. "I'm so sorry, I wasn't thinking ... I just—"

"It's okay," I cut in, not wanting the mood to sour further. I forced a smile, even though the moment had dredged up a memory that I preferred to leave untouched. "I would get upset, but these pancakes are too good."

My attempt at humor worked. Jesse relaxed, and Betty gave me a grateful smile before turning back to her plate.

"He's gotten better at this over the years," she said with a playful glint in her eye. "When we were kids, he used to burn everything he touched."

I laughed, stealing a glance at Jesse, who was busy cutting a pancake for Bisera. "Hard to imagine."

"Oh, believe me," Betty continued, "he's still not much of a cook. But he's improved since then. Mostly out of necessity, I think."

Jesse finally looked up, raising an eyebrow in mock offense. "I'm right here, you know."

Betty shrugged, completely unbothered. "I'm just telling her the truth. I'd say you've gotten about as good as a man living on his own can get."

"How often do you get to come home, anyway?" I asked, genuinely curious as I sipped my coffee.

Betty answered before Jesse could. "Not often. He's always traveling. We've had to practically drag him back for Bisera's birthdays."

Jesse gave her a look, but it was softened by a smile. "It's not that bad."

"Not that bad?" Betty echoed, her tone teasing. "He announced his engagement three years ago, when he was working in Dubai, and never even brought the girl home!"

"Dubai?" I asked. "Who was the lucky lady?"

"Oh, she was Macedonian, of course," Betty said with a smirk. "You can't escape us, even in Dubai. But it didn't work out."

"That's a story for another time," Jesse interjected, though his voice was light, as if the memory didn't bother him. "Speaking of engagements," he looked at Betty, "Sasha is getting married."

Betty's reaction was almost dismissive. "He is? Oh well."

"He's her first boyfriend," Jesse explained. "I'm invited, by the way."

"Enjoy yourself, and please, don't say hi from me."

"Sasha Andov?" I asked remembering an invitation I received a couple of weeks ago.

Both Jesse and Betty answered at the same time. "Yes."

"Do you know him?" Jesse asked.

"Yeah, he's a distant relative from Stefan's father's side. I'm invited, too."

"Well," Betty said, her tone half-joking, "I hope you both get drunk and puke on the cake."

Jesse shook his head, "So much for not holding a grudge."

"Considering the fact that my whole family is invited, I'll probably skip that wedding," I said pressing my lips together.

There was a brief pause, a subtle shift in the atmosphere. Jesse looked at me with a wordless acknowledgment, and I couldn't help but wonder what he was thinking at that moment. Was it about the countless times I'd spoken of my family in a negative light? Or perhaps about his own experiences with them? Or maybe it was the realization that I would be missing the wedding celebration for such a ridiculous reason.

"Oh, I hear you," Betty said, breaking the silence with a lighthearted tone. "We can get together for another pancake session instead."

"I won't ever trust you to feed Ilaria with your pancakes," Jesse teased, turning to me with a grin. "Believe me, better take out."

I watched their playful banter—Betty tousling Jesse's hair in retaliation, Jesse debating with Milan whether the perfect filling for a pancake was Nutella or raspberry jam, Milan and Bisera competing for who can manage a bigger bite—and a wave of gratitude washed over me for this unexpected turn in my morning. Yet, a pang struck my chest, a twinge of regret that this wasn't my everyday reality, that this delightfully warm episode would inevitably end.

But then, almost as quickly, the tension eased, and I found it easier to breathe. I remembered that tomorrow was Friday. And on Friday night, there would be Igor Džambazov's concert.

4

JESSE'S CAR WAS PARKED a little way down the street from my house, the engine still humming softly as we sat in silence. Neither of us seemed in any hurry to move. The rush to escape the downpour had left us both slightly damp—my hair clung to the sides of my face, and his shirt was darker at the shoulders where the rain had soaked through.

The memory of the concert was still vivid, the phantom bass notes still resonating through my core.

Just a couple of hours ago, the square had been alive with energy, the air electric with anticipation as we joined the crowd. There was something liberating about being lost in that sea of people, jumping, singing along, and exchanging "this is the time of our lives" glances.

The whole experience felt like a hazy, feverish dream—so much so that I forgot I was thirty-two and that there was someone in my life I was responsible for. It happens to parents sometimes when they know their kid is safe somewhere. I had put Milan to bed and waited until he fell asleep. Vesna was watching TV in the next room, and I knew she would check on

45

him every fifteen minutes, as she usually did, regardless of whether I was home.

But it also happens when you're so immersed in a moment, so present, that the past and future don't exist—there are only these feelings, this moment—one at a time: this one inhale, this one heartbeat.

There was a lot of that today. Us leaning in close to make our comments audible over the roar of the music. A lot of heart-warming, cheek-hurting laughter. My hand resting on his chest, feeling more at home every time I leaned in to hear what he had to say next. His fingers around my wrist, keeping my hand on his chest longer. Me climbing up the parapet to see the stage better as the band performed the only song I knew, dancing without worrying if I looked stupid or "too old for this shit," and him steadying me by the waist as I jumped down when the song was over.

And when a noisy crowd of what looked like twenty college students on summer vacation chose the area where we were standing as a passageway to the bar, Jesse's palm closed around my upper arm and pulled me back into him to avoid me being swept towards the bar with them. I glanced back at him, mouthing "thank you," and he just held my gaze. He smelled like fresh rain on dry earth, mixed with the subtle spice of cedar, grounding me in his presence and making me wish the place would get even more crowded.

I didn't even question myself, didn't wonder why I felt this way or whether I was even allowed to. That voice started grumbling in my head a couple of times, but I shut it down.

Just for one night. It feels so good—when will you get to experience all this again?

There was a lot of unplanned and situational hand-holding, too. Like when Jesse said, "Let's go get you something else. The waitstaff isn't making it to us," taking my hand and leading me through the throng of people to reach the bar. His grip was firm but gentle, guiding me through the crush of bodies, and it felt painfully familiar, like something I hadn't experienced for an indecently long time. I felt taken care of. It also felt like something as a matter of fact, like this is what hands are for, this is what *our* hands are for.

And then I saw him drinking freaking mineral water.

"Are you not drinking because you plan to drive me home again?" I asked.

He chuckled and shrugged. "I certainly will drive you home. But ... I don't really drink much."

"Wow. I've had way too many drinks in front of you over the past week, and now I feel weird about it."

Jesse smirks, his eyes crinkling at the corners. "It's not a contest. Besides," his voice drops, but I can still hear him because he's leaning in close, his lips grazing my ear, "as we've already established, you can do whatever you feel like doing without having to explain yourself."

Well, okay.

Jesse was right earlier: my relatives weren't there. At least, I didn't see anybody. I was sure there were some people who knew me, but I'd always been bad with faces, and for the first time, I thought of it as a gift. I just let myself be, without looking around in fear of being exposed.

There was one of them, though—Ivana, Stefan's cousin. In fact, she was more one of *us* than one of *them.*

She spotted Petar first, then shouted my name and rushed to hug me. She complimented my dress; I said I loved her new hair color. Then her eyes landed on Jesse, who was standing next to me.

Ivana was the only person in the family I knew wouldn't judge me, because she herself knew a thing or two about being judged. When she went to Croatia to study two years ago, dyed her hair dark, got a bad-ass side shave, and started wearing androgynous clothes, all the relatives began speculating about her orientation. They wouldn't do it openly—conversations like those usually take place behind closed doors—and I didn't even know there were talks until I overheard Vesna discussing it with a friend on the phone, using her dramatically hushed tone. That meant the situation had gotten out of hand.

No, Ivana would never judge me for taking what I want.

As if to confirm my thoughts, she gave Jesse a once-over and shouted in my ear, "God, he's hot. I hope you make the most out of it."

And it felt like a cobblestone-heavy weight was lifted off my chest, and a small, shy thought made its way into my prefrontal cortex: *maybe I should.*

Then, suddenly, it started raining—heavy droplets splattering all over the ground, turning the asphalt black. Jesse grabbed my hand again, and we ran toward the parking lot to the sound of rain and the bewildered screams of the crowd.

I asked him to stop the car a hundred feet before our house, for the same old reason. And there we were, sitting in the dark of his Kia, deafened by the raindrops splattering against the windshield. Jesse shifted slightly in his seat, and as he turned to face me, his gaze dropped to my arm. I followed his eyes, realizing that the scar on my forearm had caught his attention. It was a week-old scar, a faded red oval, a reminder of a clumsy oven accident. Before I could say anything, he reached out and gently took my hand, his touch sending a shiver up my arm.

His fingers were warm as they traced the outline of the scar, his touch soft, almost reverent. "Where did this come from?" he asked, his voice low, filled with genuine curiosity.

I managed a faint smile. "You should see the chicken."

Jesse's laughter was soft, a warm rumble that filled the car, and I found myself laughing too, though it felt like a fragile thing, teetering on the edge of something much more intense. I took a quiet breath, trying to ease the tension that was now coursing through my entire body.

Jesse's hand still held mine, and I could feel the warmth of his skin, the way his thumb traced absent patterns on the back of my hand.

"Look," he began, his voice quiet, almost hesitant, "it doesn't have to be weird."

I didn't respond, just kept my eyes on him, my heart in my throat.

He continued, searching my face for any sign of what I might be thinking. "I'm not trying to come onto you."

His words took me by surprise, and where there was supposed to be a sense of relief, something else stung me. "You aren't?"

He smiled, a little sadly. "I mean, you're straight-up gorgeous, obviously—duh. But ... you've probably faced too many inappropriate encounters recently. I'm not going to be one of them."

I looked down at the gear shift, the storage compartment filling up the space between us, a wave of conflicting emotions crashing over me. There was gratitude, yes, but there was also something else—something that felt like regret, like a missed opportunity, like the loss of something I hadn't even realized I wanted until now.

"It's just ..." he continued, his voice soft, "I've learned that my visits home don't necessarily have to be a terrible experience. And it's mostly because of you. It turns out I really like hanging out with you."

His words sent a jolt of warmth through me, but they also made me feel incredibly vulnerable. I wanted to say something, anything, to fill the silence, but all I could do was keep looking down, feeling the weight of his gaze on me.

"You look disappointed," he said.

I hesitated, my mind racing. Did I want this? Did I want to cross this line? But then the answer came, clear and undeniable, and it was enough to make me lift my gaze to meet his, my heart pounding in my chest.

"Maybe that's because I wanted ..." I began, my voice barely a whisper, "you to come onto me."

His expression shifted, surprise flickering across his face, quickly followed by something deeper, more intense. His eyes darkened, and I could see the struggle in them, the way he was trying to hold himself back, to keep control.

"Well, then," he murmured, his voice low and rough with something that made my pulse quicken, "I take it back."

And before I could process the words, before I could say anything in response, he was leaning in, closing the distance between us. His hand found my waist, as his lips met mine in a kiss that stole the breath from my lungs.

The world outside the car vanished. All I could feel was him—the heat of his body, the way his other hand slid up to cradle my face, his touch gentle yet insistent. The kiss was nothing like I had imagined; it was more—more intense, more consuming, more everything.

His lips moved against mine with a hunger that matched my own. A realization settled deep in my stomach—every time he watched me eat, this is what he had been imagining—how he would devour my mouth, drinking me in. The thought made heat surge through me. My hands slid to his rain-soaked shoulders, pulling him closer as I deepened the kiss.

When he pulled back, it was only for a breath, and then he was kissing me again, deeper this time, more urgent. The rain continued to pound against the car, but it was a distant sound, drowned out by the rush of blood in my ears, the rapid thudding of my heart.

I let myself get lost in the feeling of being wanted, of being needed. I let myself forget the world outside, forget the past, forget everything except the man in front of me and the way he was making me feel.

But then the reality of the situation started to creep back in, and I slowly pulled away, my breath coming in ragged gasps. Jesse's eyes were dark all over, his chest rising and falling rapidly as he looked at me, searching my face for any sign of regret.

But I didn't regret it. Not even for a second. I just ... needed to think, needed to process what had just happened, what it meant.

"Ilaria ..." Jesse's voice was soft, hesitant, as if he was afraid of breaking whatever spell had been cast between us.

I looked at him, my heart still racing, and for a moment, all I could do was stare, trying to catch my breath, trying to find the words to explain what I was feeling. But nothing came.

And I smiled at him, as reassuring as I could, hoping he would understand that this wasn't a rejection, that this wasn't the end of whatever had just started between us.

Then, without another word, I pulled the door handle and ran out into the rain, knowing he was watching me until I entered the house. I stood behind the door for what felt like an eternity, panting, water dripping off me onto the doormat.

There was a new man in my life, and everything about him was unfamiliar—his hands moved with a different rhythm, he smelled different, he tasted different. The strangeness of it all terrified me, the way his presence felt both foreign and magnetic.

Jesse and I had found a connection fast, but it was more than just an understanding—it was something primal, like a force that pulled us together before we could think it through. It moved beyond words, beyond shared stories and familiar laughter. It lived in the space between us, where instinct spoke louder than anything we could ever say. And that pull, raw and animalistic, was so powerful it scared me.

As I took my sandals off still feeling light-headed, I heard Jesse's car pass by, driving away. And I suddenly realized that this, him—felt like something I wouldn't be able to just walk away from.

5

"SHIT, IT'S HIM," I muttered, staring at the phone in my hand as it rang. I was at my only non-Macedonian friend Nina's place, having just shared last night's events with her in vivid detail. She was the only one who would ever get excited about something like this—maybe a little too excited, given that her own love life was quieter than mine these days. I wondered if that's why I came to her in the first place. "What should I do?" I mouthed as if Jesse could hear me before I pressed the damn green thing.

"Answer it, answer it!" Nina urged, nearly bouncing in her seat, clearly enjoying this new thing happening in my life, maybe more than she should.

I took a deep breath and picked up, trying to keep my voice steady. "Hello?"

"Hey," Jesse's voice came through, soft and familiar, though with a hint of uncertainty. "How are you?"

"I'm ... good. You?"

"Yeah, good. Listen," Jesse began, "it's a long weekend, so I was thinking ... What do you say we take the kids to Ohrid?"

"Ohrid?" I repeated, caught off guard. "Like … overnight?"

"Two rooms," he clarified, and I could almost hear the smile in his voice, sensing what I was implying.

I exhaled, feeling a bit of the tension ease. "What did Betty say?" I asked, trying to ground myself in the moment.

Jesse chuckled softly. "Betty would sell her soul for some sleep. She actually asked if we could stay there for a week."

I squeezed out a nervous laugh and glanced over at Nina, who was practically holding her breath, eyes wide with excitement. She whispered, "I can keep the kids here while you two are in Ohrid."

I threw a piece of arugula at her from the salad bowl, and she rolled off her chair, laughing.

"Where are you?" Jesse asked, sounding curious.

"At my *former* friend's place," I replied, glaring at Nina. "So … did you check the hotel availability?" I asked, trying to sound confident.

"Don't worry about it. I know a guy in Ohrid who owns a hotel our company built for him. He'll get us the rooms, no problem."

"Well …"

"And don't worry about any expenses. I'm inviting you guys, I'll take care of everything."

"No, really, that's not …"

"You know I won't take your money, so can you just go with it?"

Nina had climbed back onto her chair, nodding at me like a gigantic bobblehead.

I stood up and paced around the room. "Is it tomorrow?"

"Tomorrow," he confirmed. "We'll be back by Monday evening. Unless you have something else planned …"

"No, it's just … Are you sure you want to spend your weekend with two kids?" I asked, already making a mental list of what I'd need to pack for Milan and imagining how challenging it might be to manage two energetic kids by the water.

Without hesitation, Jesse went straight to the core of it. "I want to spend my weekend with *you*." I held my breath, feeling my heart flutter. His ability to call a spade a spade was quickly becoming my favorite thing about this man.

Maybe even higher on my list than the way his hands felt on my waist.

"I'm sure the kids are going to love it too," Jesse's tone was light and warm. I could almost picture him sitting across from me, smiling, reaching for my hand. "I'm just combining a good deed with pleasure."

I moved as far from Nina as I could and quietly asked, "What kind of pleasure are we talking about?"

His low laughter reverberated through my spine. "I thought I mentioned there will be two rooms. I only mean the pleasure of your company, Ilaria." Then, as if realizing how it sounded and what I had told him last night trembling like a flimsy leaf under his gaze, he quickly added, "Unless you have other expectations ... In that case, we can reconsider. But that wasn't my intention. I just want to get away, drive far, and make some memories."

Smooth.

Nina was staring at me so intensely, I thought her eyes might pop out of her head. I bit my lip, my mind swirling with thoughts and images. Ohrid really was the perfect place to make memories. A shimmering lake framed by rugged mountains, ancient churches perched on cliffs, and cobblestone streets that seemed to whisper centuries-old secrets. Waterfront restaurants, sprawling parks, and the lake promenade lined with local sweets stalls and boat rentals. After countless visits, instead of growing tired of the place, I found myself falling more in love with it every time. The thought of watching the kids splash in the clear, cool waters, their laughter mingling with the gentle lapping of waves against the shore ...

Oh no. I'm going to have to wear a bikini.

"Okay," I finally said, wincing. "But I'll take a taxi and meet you at the gas station."

If he protests and insists on picking us up from home, I will remind him that the last thing I need is to give a free show to my asshole housemates. Let them die trying to figure out where I am headed with my suitcase.

But he just said, "Fine."

"No argument?"

"I choose my battles."

As we hung up, I looked at Nina, who was grinning from ear to ear. "It looks like," I said, trying to sound casual, "I need a new swimsuit."

·   ·   ·

When I was working in India, six of us girls lived together in our Goan apartment. We spent seven months a year there, cooking together, cleaning whenever necessary, stocking the fridge without any set rules, and waking each other up for early morning excursions. The dishes were washed by whoever found them in the sink, and the trash was taken out by whoever was already dressed and standing at the door. Some of us were too loud, others too reserved; some were vegetarians, others fast food enthusiasts; some were in their twenties, while others were pushing forty.

In all the three seasons I spent in India, and the twenty years before that, I never had as many issues with roommates as I did with this "family."

They say relationships sour when you have to fight for territory.

Not that my relatives were openly trying to drive me out of the shared home. I don't believe they ever secretly wanted that either—it was more about showing who was in charge, a strange eagerness to emphasize who was older and demanded respect. At first, I didn't notice anything because I was learning the traditions by watching these people. I thought, "If they do it this way, it must be right." I told myself. "Danche is just sensitive, anxious, controlling." That's who she was; it couldn't be easy for her to live with such wild and messy creatures like us. Sometimes Milan and I would go catch frogs (only to release them later), and when we returned, I'd have to wash him down with a hose in the yard. If I missed a spot and Milan went upstairs to play with his cousins, Danche would immediately send him home "to get clean."

I was sure it was because she was afraid her white couch would get stained.

Their space was always spotless, the children taught to be orderly before they were even potty-trained. They would come over to ours to have pillow fights and set up Play-Doh exhibits on the dining table.

But on her own turf, Danche didn't allow such chaos—after all, guests could drop by at any moment. And God forbid they find their living room messy and report to the town's gossip network that Danche failed at housekeeping for once!Later, I realized that her insecurity and habit of bending the rules to suit herself made her one of those people who coax you into an open conversation, gather information, record it in their mental diary, and then use it against you at the opportune moment. A constant readiness to assume superiority and rub it in your face.

For example, once during a family gathering, I mentioned that I wasn't particularly close with my sister which never stopped me from building sisterly relationships with my friends. It was a relaxed conversation around the table; there were many of us, and we were discussing whether one should have a second child just to ensure the first wouldn't grow up alone. I shared my experience: my sister had to take care of me when I was born, and I doubt she was grateful to our mother for that childhood. A couple of years later, during a heated argument, Danche suddenly threw at me:

"You and your sister aren't close; that's why you and I aren't close—you don't get close with your family members. I'd never stood a chance with you anyway."

Wow, bitch. I'm not close with my sister because there's a thirteen-year age gap and almost nothing in common, not because we had a falling out or despised each other, and certainly not because she tried to impose some absurd idea of seniority on me.

But that came later—those first few years in that house, I spent in blissful ignorance. I tried to be a good sister-in-law. The breaking point came when the brothers had a serious falling out because Lazar refused to let Stefan return to the family business that Stefan had founded, declaring, "Give me twenty thousand euros, and you can come back."

It was never about money for Stefan. He had blindly handed over the entire company to his brother—along with all the active client contracts and the reputation they had spent fifteen years building. That year, Lazar received half of the revenue—five thousand euros—as he walked away to try something new. But he never once attempted to remain a co-owner on paper or sell his share to his brother—he simply gave it to him. Along with the clients who would continue to provide for him and his children for years to come.

"Give me twenty thousand euros, and you can come back."

Stefan had been a good brother. As I later learned from the flood of stories that poured out of him after the ugly argument—stories he had kept to himself for years to maintain good relations between me and them (because he knew I'd hate them if I saw them through his eyes)—Stefan had forgiven his brother for countless minor slights and years of belittling remarks and condescending behavior. Lazar always spoke, acted, and even carried himself at the dining table as if he were more important, smarter, the true head of the family. Meanwhile, Stefan—well into his thirties—was still treated like a clueless teenager, incapable of taking care of his family or business. He had always let it slide: *"He's my brother—that's why."*

The twenty thousand euros was the last straw, something that couldn't be written off as carelessness. It was clear that this wasn't a slip of the tongue or a mistake, but a character trait, and worse, the most accurate and telling illustration of his attitude toward his brother.

And suddenly, all those incidents I had previously overlooked resurfaced in my memory like wine corks bobbing in the sea. I wanted to talk to them about everything, I wanted to know their perspective, I wanted to go through the list and cross off each point.

But they just looked at me as if I had made it all up. "Family is the most important thing in life," they said. "Family is all we have, and we must stick together." Danche was ready to keep smiling as if she hadn't heard my questions, and I was supposed to smile back as if I could step back into blissful ignorance.

I had a friend, one of those couples' friends Stefan and I hung out with, who once said, "Even if I know someone is badmouthing me behind my back, I'll still sit down with them at the table, eat, drink, and laugh because they didn't say it to my face, so there's no conflict."

I then realized that this was a level of assimilation into the local customs that I was not capable of. The truth was that if she stopped sitting at the table with everyone who talked about her behind her back, she'd be completely alone, and she couldn't afford that. I, on the other hand, could. Easy-peasy, second nature.

What I couldn't do was go to Danche's place and smile at her sisters and parents, knowing that half an hour earlier, she had been slamming me behind my back to her own family.

Letting go of that circus was as easy for me as taking the first breath after a long, suffocating sleep. And I realized that if I couldn't be honest, I would only say things that conformed to their rules of politeness but were not lies either. It turned out that the only thing that fit within this paradigm was "hello." Not a word more did they hear from me, except for those rare occasions when the veil of "decent neighbors" was lifted, and they could tolerate an honest exchange.

Like on Saturday morning, when I was preparing to leave for Ohrid. Everything was ready: I'd stuffed both Milan's and my backpacks with the things that were supposedly enough to keep us clean, entertained, sun-blocked and mosquito-protected for two days. I'd even made some hot dog puffs for the road, and now was scrubbing the baking tray in the yard sink when I heard Danche shaking a carpet on the second-floor terrace right above my head. I looked up at her through the dust and debris floating down on me.

A voice in the back of my head whispered. It's such a great illustration of how I feel the whole time I'm in this place. Me looking up at her shaking her carpet above my freshly washed hair.

I somehow knew that if it was Milan in my place, she'd waited. In fact, I'd seen her wait. Or ask him to move away "so that auntie Danche doesn't dust you, baby!" Kids were everything in this culture, you would come across as a complete dickhead if you reprimand somebody else's child, not mentioning shake your carpet on their head.

Nobody would judge her for dusting *me* though.

"Could you at least wait until I finish?" I called up, trying to keep my tone calm, but there was no mistaking the edge in my voice.

"It isn't getting to you," Danche replied, glancing down at me as if I was making a big deal out of nothing.

"It sure *is* getting to me," I shot back, feeling the tension in my chest rise.

She shrugged, her tone still dripping with indifference. "Well, where am I supposed to shake them? You didn't want me to do it from the main terrace."

"Of course I didn't. It's not like you offer to clean it up afterwards. Or to re-wash Milan's clothes that'd been drying there?"

"You know," she said, tugging her white carpet off the railing, "this yard is shared. I have the right to shake my carpets here. Just because you live on the ground floor, you seem to think you have some kind of ownership over the whole area."

She said it with the expression she always wore when she assumed the role of the elder sister—the one, as we had long established, that had been sorely absent from my aimless and dowry-less life. It was an expression of selflessness and sacrificial honesty, tinged with the kind of maternal impatience and noble fatigue in her sad green eyes. The same look she'd had when she set her potted palms exactly where Milan and I liked to play football, or when she decided my woodpile needed reorganizing to free up space in the yard. Or, more pointedly, when she hinted that I shouldn't speak to my child in a foreign language, because she was convinced I might be saying something bad about her and getting away with it.

Did she really just say I think I have some kind of ownership over the whole area?

That's when I saw red.

"I don't feel like I own anything at all in this house," I shot back. "I pay half the bills, but it doesn't feel like I own an inch. I'm sharing a floor with our mother-in-law—who, let me remind you, is also yours—while you stretch yourself across an entire floor. I don't even have access to the attic because the only entrance is through *your* room!"

"You should be grateful we built that floor!" Danche's voice took on a sanctimonious edge. "Where would we all be living now?"

"Excuse you? Did you just say *you built that floor?* Am I losing my mind, or did you only add one damn room up there? *One!*" My voice rose, my face flushed with frustration. "The floor with three bedrooms and two bathrooms was built by our father-in-law long before you ever met Lazar. Let's not forget, Stefan owned a third of that space—it was his inheritance from his father. And he gave it it to *you*. So, no, I don't know where I'd be living, but I'm damn sure *you* wouldn't be up there if my husband hadn't been generous enough to give up his rights."

She gasped. "I invested fifteen thousand euros into that construction!"

I squinted. "Funny how you never mention how much the company—still co-owned by Stefan at the time—invested in that construction."

"I'd love to see you back that up with receipts," Danche shot back, flashing her signature crooked smile—the one she wore when she thought she had the upper hand. In my experience, there were only moments between that smile and the inevitable tears of righteousness.

"There are no receipts, my dear, because both Lazar and Stefan had to do compensatory work for the company that sent the trucks of sand and bricks to finish the second floor. The same company that provided the metal fence that still shines on your terrace after all these years. Stefan paid your bills with his own labor—fixing motors with his bare hands—so that years later, you could stand here and claim he never contributed to the place you live in. You ungrateful piece of work!"

Lazar appeared in the doorway, looking down at me with a frown that seemed out of place on his usually easygoing, salesman's face. His fair hair ruffled in the breeze, but that frown—a look I'd come to know too well—was reserved just for me.

"What's your problem?" he asked, his tone heavy with accusation, even though he'd barely heard a word of the argument. Danche, meanwhile, was already playing the victim, her lower lip trembling just enough to garner sympathy.

"You're my problem," I muttered under my breath, snatching up the baking tray from the sink. I spun on my heel and stormed back into the house.

Before I even realized what I was doing, I had my phone in my hand, Jesse's number ringing. "I changed my mind," I said the moment he answered. "You can pick me up from home."

On autopilot, I finished packing, told Milan to get dressed, and quickly changed my own clothes, making sure I hadn't forgotten my charger and double-checking if the mosquito repellent I'd brought also protected against ticks. All the while, on the second screen, my mind replayed the latest argument and all the ones that came before it, generating counterarguments like some kind of chatGPT.

Stefan used to say, "It's your house, too." But the very fact that he had to say it is eloquent enough. I'd never felt like home here, it was always a temporary solution for us. But please give the Nobel Prize to the one who declared that there's nothing more permanent than temporary.

I'd just said more than I ever intended, but the funny part was that I kind of wanted to say more. There was this greedy combative monster growing inside of me, and the only thing I was thinking was: will I be able to hold it down or will it eventually take over? And when it does, will I finally feel a relief?

From my terrace, I watched as Jesse got out of the car and strode confidently toward me, his expression calm. But when his gaze met mine, there was a subtle shift—not enough for our audience to notice, but just enough for me to see. The faintest trace of warmth flickered across his face, a small comfort in the midst of this chaos.

Without a word, he grabbed our backpacks and stowed them in the trunk.

"Come on, Milan! We're leaving," I called out, my voice steady, though I felt anything but.

Milan came running from the house, his face lighting up with excitement at the sight of Jesse's car. "Yay! We're riding in the Kia again!" he exclaimed, his enthusiasm infectious.

"Hey, Milan," Jesse greeted him with a smile as he closed the trunk. "Get in! Bisera's already in the car."

"Bisera!" Milan shouted, bouncing on his toes with glee.

Jesse turned toward the upper terrace, where Lazar and Danche stood, their expressions unreadable. "Good morning," he said, his tone polite but distant which somehow made even a more pronounced statement.

Lazar responded with a curt nod, while Danche's lips thinned into a tight line.

As Jesse opened the door for me, we exchanged a quiet smile and I felt his hand gently rest on the small of my back. It wasn't just a touch—it was a reminder. For the first time in forever, I realized I wasn't alone. He was on my team. I mean, *he really was on my team of all the possible teams*. And it felt safe.

As we were driving away, I said, "Sorry about that. I kind of used you to show off. It was childish."

Jesse glanced at me, a smile playing at the corner of his lips. "If anything, I was the one showing off."

I gave him a grateful look feeling the tension leaving my body.

"I take it something happened at home?" He asked, his tone gentle but probing.

"Nothing new."

"Well then, it was a great idea to get you some fresh air and nice views."

"I thought the idea was to take the kids out," I said, nodding toward the back where Milan was now pretending to be a race car driver and Bisera was her enthusiastic co-pilot.

Jesse grinned slyly. "Just like you said last time: we go where we need to go, and the kids just tag along, right?"

I finally took a good look at him—he was wearing a light blue T-shirt that fit him perfectly, highlighting his broad shoulders and toned arms. His sunglasses sat casually on the bridge of his nose, framing his face in a way that made him look innately handsome. I let out a deep breath, realizing just how much time we'd have ahead of us—two and a half hours of driving, four of us crammed in one car, and then two days of trying to juggle new roles while pleasing each other. Though, in reality, it would mostly be Jesse and me trying to keep two little manipulative shitheads happy.

"So, did we get the hotel?" I asked, half-expecting him to say there'd been a complication.

"Yes, two adjacent rooms with a lake view. Playground and swimming pool included. Three hundred feet from the beach."

"Wow. You must have built that guy one hell of a hotel," I teased.

"You'll see it for yourself soon enough. Are you ready for a dip?" he asked, his voice warm with amusement.

"Oh, I can't swim."

"You can't?" He glanced at me, surprise evident even through his sunglasses.

"Nope. I'm afraid of water."

"Really? Didn't you live near the beach for a few years?"

I paused, a little surprised he remembered that. I'd mentioned it casually over drinks at that Turkish café. "I did. But ... I don't know, it's irrational. I guess I've always been afraid this big nothingness would just swallow me up."

Even saying it made me want to gulp down air like I was about to dive into the deep blue abyss, knowing full well it wouldn't be up to me if I ever came back up.

Jesse didn't respond right away. His expression grew thoughtful, and he kept his eyes on the road, processing my words.

"Milan can swim though," I added after a beat. "Stefan taught him when he was really little."

"Wow. How do you handle that?"

"What do you mean?"

"Letting him swim when you're probably terrified the moment you see him in the water?"

I blinked. It was a damn good question, one that hit closer to home than I expected. "I just ... try to separate my fears from his. He's not afraid, so I force myself to stay put and let him live his life."

His glance flickered between me and the road a couple of times, and I could swear there was admiration in his eyes, but I couldn't tell for sure because of the damn sunglasses. "You don't have to go in the water," he finally said reassuringly. "I'll handle it. We'll have fun either way."

And I already was. In the back, Milan and Bisera were playing "I spy with my little eye," giggling over each guess. They had moved on to devouring my hot dog puffs, the crinkling of the bag mixing with their laughter. Jesse's strong hands rested on the steering wheel, guiding the car as though it was an extension of himself—his movements were so fluid, so natural. His presence, calm yet vibrant, filled the car in a way that made me feel grounded.

In his company, I didn't feel the need to hold my heart tightly, didn't have to fidget or overthink. My mind was quiet, my body at peace. I let myself relax into that feeling, the tension melting from my shoulders as I leaned back into the seat.

At some point, I must've drifted off. I remember hearing the kids start chanting nursery rhymes, their small voices blending together in a sweet, chaotic melody. And then, I could swear I heard Jesse's deep voice humming along with them.

6

I HAD HEARD THAT Ohrid emptied out in winter. But now, in July, it was a magnet for German backpackers, groups of Asian tourists, and Macedonians who could afford the unjustifiably expensive holidays with a view of the azure waters. I couldn't help but wonder—if the guidebooks didn't mention that this lake was a UNESCO World Heritage site, would this coffee still cost as much as an entire breakfast for two back at our "Tuscany"?

I handed Jesse the cold drink as I settled down on the towel next to him. Ten feet away, Bisera was diligently digging a moat around a lumpy, half-collapsed sandcastle, while Milan busily carried water from the lake in his little bucket. They hadn't moved an inch since I left them fifteen minutes ago under Jesse's watchful eye, while I slipped away to change into the swimsuit in the café restroom.

"Got you a coffee," I said, sitting back, the sun warm against my bare skin. "Sorry it took so long. The place was packed, and there's only one girl working the bar."

I adjusted the strap of my bikini—a deep blue I chose yesterday in the store, the only colour that looked okay on my pale skin. It wasn't one of those flashy pieces designed to turn heads, but it fit me perfectly, hugging the curves of my hips and breast. I'd never had much trouble fitting into anything, really. Maybe it was because I didn't dwell too much on my body's imperfections, or maybe because being tall and having just enough boobs meant I could make up for whatever minor flaws my figure had.

I caught Jesse glancing at me—his gaze traveled down over the line of my collarbone, across the swell of my chest in the bikini top, then moved along my thighs.

There was a familiarity now—this subtle, unspoken dance we'd fallen into over the last week. It reminded me of the first time at his place when I noticed him checking me out, that brief flicker of something more in his eyes. And here it was again, that same look. Only now, it felt different, more intentional, like we both knew the game we were playing.

He cleared his throat, "I'm sure if there had been a guy working the bar, you'd have gotten your order without waiting in line."

My brows furrowed as I waited for him to elaborate. His sunglasses were perched on the edge of his nose, and when he leaned in slightly, his smile deepened, adding a playful glint to his brown eyes as he spoke.

"You're the most stunning woman on this whole beach," he said, his voice dropping just enough to send a pleasant warmth through me. It was the way he said it, like it was a fact rather than a compliment—his tone soft but confident, making it impossible to brush off.

I stared at him for a beat too long, my heart doing a little flip in my chest before I finally found my voice. "Well, then," I said, shifting my weight on the towel, "maybe next time you should be the one going for the coffee."

He raised an eyebrow, clearly intrigued. "Why's that?"

I shot him a sideways glance, deliberately letting my eyes drift over his bare torso, lingering on the smooth planes of his chest and the broad expanse of his shoulders, strong and sun-kissed, as if to make it clear what I was referring to. His lips curled into a grin, clearly catching my meaning.

"If the trick is being the most stunning person on the beach," I said, "I'm sure you could charm the girl behind the bar into giving you free ice cream."

Jesse let out a laugh, half-bewildered, half-amused, his eyes lighting up as he realized I could play this game just as well as he could.

"Excuse me, but I've never flirted for food before. I draw the line at shameless snack-seducing."

"C'mon, Jesse! You flirted for rooms with a good view, and you draw the line at ice-cream?"

He snickered. "Okay, just to be clear, I didn't flirt for the rooms. I pulled some strings. Though, now that you mention it, maybe I should have—I could've scored us a spa day, too."

I grinned. "Think you could flirt us a free babysitter while you're at it?"

He clicked his tongue, "Eh, I don't know. I kinda like doing it myself."

"Yeah," I kinda liked it, too.

A pause fell between us, a comfortable silence as we watched the kids. Their banter mingled with the gentle rush of the waves, light and carefree. Milan had dropped his toy shovel while distracted, and Bisera, ever the opportunist, swooped in with a mischievous glint in her eye.

"Milan, look what I found!" she chimed, holding up the shovel like it was treasure.

Milan reached for it, but Bisera pulled it back, her lip jutting out in an exaggerated pout. "You don't really need this, do you? How about you give me your bucket instead? Pleeease?" Her voice was sweet, dripping with that innocent charm only a five-year-old could pull off.

Milan hesitated, frowning a little but clearly unsure. "But ... it's my favorite bucket," he protested weakly.

Bisera's eyes widened, and her pout deepened as she clutched the shovel close to her chest, giving him the full force of her wide-eyed gaze. "But I need it more. I will give it back," she insisted, batting her eyelashes for good measure.

Jesse chuckled beside me. "She's laying it on thick."

I smirked, watching Milan finally cave with a sigh, handing over the bucket with a resigned, "Okay, fine."

"She's learning early," I said, shaking my head with a smile. "Poor Milan won't stand a chance when she's older."

Jesse chuckled softly, his gaze lingering on Bisera for a moment before he turned back to me, his expression relaxed but attentive, as if he were still thinking about our conversation.

"So," I began, raising my hand to shield my eyes from the sun as I glanced over at Jesse, "the only thing I know about your job is that you work in construction. What is it exactly that you do?"

"In very official and boring language, I'm a business development manager," he said. "It means I focus on closing deals, securing new projects, building relationships with clients."

"But you seem to know your tech side well," I added, the puzzle pieces slowly falling into place.

"Yeah, I'm an engineer. But somehow I like dealing with people more than with specs."

I nodded. "You like reading them and giving them what they want."

I said it like I'd just cracked some secret code, but the moment I spoke, I saw the shift in his eyes. He understood where I was going with this, the suggestion that maybe he could read me just as easily.

"That can be true. But it's not what's going on here," he looked right at me, his tone changing from casual to serious as he added, "I have no idea what *you* want, Ilaria."

His words hung in the air between us, and for a split second, I didn't know how to respond. It wasn't playful banter anymore. There was something more in his tone, a quiet honesty that threw me off balance.

"Maybe that's what makes it interesting for you," I said, my voice quieter now, trying to keep things light, even though I could feel the weight of his words pressing against me.

"It's not …" He started, but before he could finish, Bisera's voice rang out across the sand.

"Uncle Jesse! Let's go swim!"

His jaw tensed slightly as he turned toward the sound of Bisera calling him, but then he glanced back at me, his eyes darkened with something unresolved— as if he hated leaving the conversation unfinished but knew he had no choice. His gaze lingered on mine, a wordless plea for me to wait, to hold on to what he was about to say.

"Hold that thought," he said, his voice quieter now, before heading toward the water.

I watched him go, a sudden fear creeping in—fear that this might be too fragile to move further. Of course, he didn't know what I wanted—how could he, when I wasn't even sure myself? Stefan had been a traditionalist; he believed in forever, and over time, I learned to think that way too. Eventually, I grew to love the idea that I had found him, that we were meant for each other. He had always known what he wanted, always known what he wanted to give me. I had been his priority, and I learned to accept those gifts of fate with gratitude.

Nina used to say, "Be glad you're married—out in the dating world, you can't go anywhere without pepper spray or a silver cross." And that's exactly what I did: I embraced him in the evenings and felt thankful. I knew what tomorrow would bring. I knew how my life would unfold until the very last day.

But now I sat on a beach, gazing at a view I hadn't seen since I last felt safe and certain, and I had no idea what any of this meant anymore. Do I need that silver cross now, simply because I've grown too comfortable, too used to trusting the man beside me by default? Jesse likely means no harm—and while I watched him effortlessly he handle two small children in the water, remembering how thoughtful he was to me the entire time, I knew he couldn't possibly have ill intentions. But what if I'm just another project to him, something his business mind wants to break down into tasks and turn into a success story?

To my horror, there was one thing I feared more than having my suspicions confirmed: the thought that I might never see the other side of him, the side that's not mine yet. The full-throttle Jesse—the all-consuming, head-spinning, earth-moving force he's holding back just because he doesn't know if I want him to use it to make me happy.

We didn't get a chance to return to that conversation, maybe for the best.

As he'd promised, Jesse took on water supervision while I tackled snack and sunscreen duty and bathroom trips. Three hours and four gjevreks later, and with two pounds of sand clinging to us in every possible crevice, the grown-ups were exhausted and the kids were hyped-up. We soon realized that none of us could possibly sit out the lakeside dinner Jesse had originally planned. The unanimous decision was to retreat to the hotel and order chebapi to the room.

The hotel was a charming four-star spot—modern yet inviting. Jesse, familiar with every corner, casually mentioned during check-in how the owner had originally insisted on building an extravagant rooftop deck, but Jesse suggested a more practical terrace design to preserve the charm without blowing the budget. "He thanks me for talking him out of it every time we speak," he added with a grin.

Our two adjoining rooms were spacious and well-appointed. The first thing I noticed was the large windows, perfectly framing the lake view like a postcard come to life. The décor was simple but tasteful, featuring wooden furniture, plush bedding, and soft neutral tones. Everything we needed to comfortably spend two days with the kids was there—a small table for snacks and a ginormous plasma TV in each room, plenty of space for their toys and crayons, and lots of extra towels and bedding. I especially appreciated the pull-out couch, a backup plan in case Milan, known for his restlessness at night, made sleeping in our double bed unbearable.

We had left the door between the rooms open because, unsurprisingly, Milan and Bisera had immediately gathered in my room, sprawled out in front of the TV.

I stepped out onto the terrace, feeling the warmth of the evening air as it clung to my skin. A soft breeze carried the faint sounds of distant chatter from the swimming pool area. Jesse appeared beside me, a towel slung over his shoulder. When we arrived, despite my overwhelming desire to ask the receptionist for a hose and douse both kids with dish soap in the hotel yard, I summoned my patience and washed them, one after the other, in the shower before I gave myself a good rinse. Now, Jesse was freshly showered too, smelling faintly of the same soap I had used but with the unmistakable hint of his own body scent. It enveloped me as he leaned on the railing next to me.

"You know," I said, nodding toward the distant shore where the evening city lights flickered across the water. "There were once houses on stilts over there."

"Where? In the old town?" he asked, glancing over.

"No, farther out, where The Bay of Bones Museum is located. People lived in stilt houses—it made life easier for those who relied on fishing. Archaeologists discovered wooden piles, tools, pottery, and other artifacts preserved beneath the lake. Just for reference, those villages existed around the time of ancient Egypt. Can you imagine? That's why I love places like this. I can almost see those people, living their lives, raising their kids right here, in the same spot where you've parked your car and connected your phone to Wi-Fi. It's like a clash of worlds. If you close your eyes, it's as if those people are still here, in some parallel universe."

As I finished, I found Jesse looking at me, his expression intrigued. "You really know your stuff."

I shrugged, smiling. "I used to dream of becoming a tour guide in Ohrid."

"Really?" His brow lifted in surprise.

"Yeah. When I was guiding tours in India, I never got tired of it."

"Why didn't you pursue it here?"

"I wasn't a citizen back then, and I would've needed a license. Now, I am a citizen ... but I'd have to go back to school for it. The Faculty of Tourism and Hospitality, to be specific."

Jesse's eyes narrowed thoughtfully. "It's here in Ohrid, right?"

I nodded. "Yeah, but it feels a bit late for that now."

He let out a soft chuckle. "You're talking like you're ancient or something. If it's something that makes you shine like that ..."

He gestured toward my face, and I figured he probably meant my involuntary smile. "Isn't that reason enough?"

I looked at him, feeling the sincerity behind his words. "Ohrid's far from home. Even if I did get the degree, I'd have to move Milan here. It's a lot."

Jesse's face softened. "But it's a seasonal job, right? Milan would have summer holidays, and you could bring him with you. Spend your summers here together."

I let the idea hang in the air, imagining it for a moment. "That does sound ideal."

He smiled. "It's perfect for someone like you."

"Someone like me?"

"Yeah. You like a change of scenery now and then. So do I. We're alike that way."

I gazed at him, processing his words. The quiet between us felt comfortable, the warm evening air heavy with the scent of lake water and the distant murmur of cartoons drifting from the next room.

After a moment, I broke the silence. "Are you really going to sell your family's vineyards?" I asked.

He hesitated, then nodded. "I guess it's inevitable. But I've been thinking of starting something new."

"Like what?"

"A rope park for kids. With climbing, paintball, you know ... something to get them outside, give them a bit of adventure."

I smiled. "That's a great idea, Jesse. Stefan and I ... we wanted to do something similar."

He turned to me, his surprise evident. "You did?"

"Yeah," I said, my voice a little wistful. "We'd talked about turning some family land into a place where kids could have real fun. There's nothing like that in our town—just boring birthday parties at restaurants. I thought Milan would love it. We had all these ideas, we even checked the prices for the paintball guns ... but then ..." My voice trailed off.

Jesse's expression softened as he shifted his weight, his shoulder brushing against mine and staying there without any intention of moving away. "It must be tough, having to rebuild your life with all those assholes vulturing around you."

I let out a small laugh. "You're not wrong. But it's getting better. It's not as hard as it was before. I'm not supposed to say that, though."

Jesse's brow furrowed. "Who says?"

"I don't know." I shrugged, smiling bitterly. "I'm sure by some weird-ass rules, I'm supposed to mourn until I die. But my mind is on Milan all the time. I want him to be okay, to not grow up traumatized. That's the only reason I haven't moved out yet. I wanted to rent an apartment, but ... Milan loves his cousins, his neighbor's kids, his grandma, and having this huge, loud family around ... I think it's good for him."

Jesse looked at me thoughtfully. "I think what he needs most is a happy mom."

I could feel the weight of his presence keenly, as if gravity itself was pulling me toward him.

"There are other things that can make me happy," I said, turning to him just a tad more, hoping he'd understand me as he unmistakably had before.

If the gesture doesn't do it, read it in my eyes, I thought, feeling my heart do a somersault in anticipation.

And he did.

He reached out, his fingers lightly brushing a strand of my hair still damp from the shower. His hand hadn't touched my skin, not yet, but the heat of it hovering so close to my neck was enough to make me catch my breath. And there it was—his face, so inviolably close that I could see just how impossibly, almost painfully, handsome he was in that determined, resolute way that only a man fully aware of himself could be. His eyes, dark with a mix of intent and hesitation, held mine as if searching for something— permission, maybe, or the same pull that was coursing through me. Then, as if he couldn't wait any longer, his thumb brushed my lower lip, his touch warm and deliberate, and slowly, he leaned in. His lips found mine in a kiss that was soft at first, tentative, as if we were learning each other's rhythms. But with each second, it deepened—our mouths opening, tongues brushing gently as we explored, savoring every little movement, every breath.

His other hand came up to my waist, pulling me just a little closer, anchoring me to him. My hands instinctively rose, one finding the back of his neck, fingers threading through the soft hair there, the other resting on his chest, feeling the fastened rise and fall of his breath. The kiss was slow but intentional, every touch, every shift deliberate. Compared to our first unplanned unexpected kiss in his car, this one was more of a statement, a declaration of intent, a way to say "I am going to take my time, I'm taking it seriously."

Then, suddenly, the world around us flickered. The lights went out, plunging the terrace into darkness. A distant murmur of surprise rose from the guests below, but it was the kids' startled scream from the next room that finally broke the spell.

The kids came running, their small feet pattering against the floor as they burst through the terrace doors, wide-eyed and clutching each other. Milan's voice trembled as he called out, "Mom! It's dark!"

I knelt to meet them, my phone already in hand. With a quick flick, the flashlight illuminated their worried faces. I pulled them both close, feeling Bisera's small hand clutching my shirt while Milan buried his head in my neck.

"It's okay, it's just a power cut," I soothed. "Nothing bad happened."

Jesse, standing beside me, suggested, "Stay here. I'll go check what's going on."

He vanished into the dark hotel halls; the outside lights were gone too, leaving us wrapped in a blanket of night. I led the kids back inside, the room eerily quiet except for their quickened breaths. It's strange how unused we are to the complete silence that descends when no engines, no fridges, no TVs, no ACs are humming in the background. A complete screeching silence.

We settled on the bed, and I placed my phone on the table so that the flashlight cast just enough light to calm the their fears.

Minutes passed before Jesse's call broke the silence. "Looks like the whole block is out. They're saying it might not be fixed until morning. I'll run to the store and grab some torches."

When he returned, about forty minutes later, I was already in his room. The kids had fallen asleep in mine, curled up in a pile of blankets, their soft breathing filling the air.

"They're out," I whispered as Jesse entered, placing the battery-powered lamps on the table. "We were talking, and before I knew it, they were both asleep."

Jesse smiled as he unpacked the rest of his haul.

"I'm sure Bisera will escape soon enough. Milan is famous for his kicking. I should've known by the way he treated my womb during those last two trimesters."

Jesse tried to stifle a laugh as he peeked into the next room. He went in to place one of the softly glowing lamps by the bed before returning and quietly shutting the door behind him.

That's when I realized where this left us. I felt excruciatingly aware that I was sitting on his bed, a space where he held all the authority. There was the couch, which he'd probably volunteer to sleep on to avoid making things awkward. Or I could go back to my room and use my own couch, which would be an even simpler way of liberating us both from the necessity of staying in the same room—albeit on different surfaces. I would make him believe I wasn't considering letting him close because kissing twice didn't establish anything. And I wasn't sure if he even wanted to make things more complicated. Maybe making out occasionally was all we could afford within the weird framework of our relationship. And maybe that was all I could muster the courage for.

I hadn't been wrapped in anyone's arms for more than a year. And before that, I'd only been wrapped in one man's arms for six years. How do I know I'm ready? How do I know I won't recoil at an unfamiliar touch, or be repulsed by the sight of someone else's naked body?

Jesse paced the room, retrieving a bottle of water from the minibar. He offered it to me, and all I could do, afraid to break the thickened silence, was give a small shake of my head. He unscrewed the cap and drank a third of the bottle in one gulp. Even in the dim light, I saw uncertainty flicker in his eyes as he glanced at me. His jaw tightened when he returned the bottle to the fridge, and his hands fidgeted, unsure where to rest now that they had nothing to hold. I knew he was just as unsure about our situation—just as lost, uncertain of what I wanted from him.

I have no idea what you want, Ilaria.

But he composed himself and moved toward the bed, sitting down beside me.

"Listen," he began, his voice lower. "About what you said earlier. It's not about me just wanting to solve you, to close the deal, if that's what you think."

Okay, I hadn't expected him to bring up our beach conversation. I'd been so tangled in my own doubts that I'd long since forgotten the comment I made about his reasons for pursuing me.

Seeing the seriousness in his eyes, I regretted ever implying there could ever be a cunning or dishonest layer to him. I shook my head softly. "Jesse, I was just—"

"No," he interrupted gently. "You turned out to be my type, alright?"

A breath caught in my throat.

"And not just my type. You're all the things I've always imagined but never found combined in one real person. Until now. It's crazy!" He half-smiled and huffed in disbelief. "Everything you do—it's ... the way you speak, the way you eat, the look in your eyes when you talk about history and the people you actually like, and honesty, and all the other important stuff. The way you fire back at my arrogant jokes and somehow manage to keep me humble without being cruel. Our sense of humour matches, our body rhythms click, and the way you kiss me ..." Jesse exhaled, as if searching for the right words. "But I know it's bad timing, and it's fucking killing me. You're not in a good place—you're mourning."

His words hung between us, raw and heavy. I'd imagined plenty of ways this evening could unfold, but not this. I never thought this man—who'd been occupying my thoughts for days— would admit to noticing me so thoroughly, and admiring what he saw. It was so much bigger than just appreciating my body in that bikini. It cut straight to my core, finding a keyhole I hadn't known existed and opening me wide.

My confession followed, one I never imagined sharing, even in the thousands of scenarios I'd played out in my head.

I met Jesse's gaze, unflinching. "I might mourn forever," my voice came out thick. "I might never be in a good place again. And this could just be a one-time thing. So what?" My tone was challenging, masking the fear behind my next question. "Would that be so terrible?"

He looked at me with a mixture of frustration and longing. His hand came up to cup my face, his eyes studying me with that familiar attentiveness. Then, with a bittersweet smile, he said, "It would probably destroy me in more ways than one, but ... no. It would be anything but terrible."

7

I WOKE TO THE SOUND of the door clicking shut and Jesse's voice murmuring, "Thanks. Keep the change," followed by the cheerful squeals of the kids. My lips tingled faintly, my body still heavy with the kind of tiredness that comes when every cell is suffused with euphoria—just as I had felt when I drifted off in Jesse's arms, the first rays of dawn spilling into the room. That could only mean one thing: I hadn't slept nearly enough.

I rolled onto my other side and stretched, letting a feline pleasure ripple through my muscles. My mind was a calm sea, and within my chest, a sense of rightness, of life's absolute fairness, bloomed. I had earned every second of last night, every touch that reminded me how my body works, every raw word he rasped in my ear, every moment of his weight on me, the roughness of his fingers closing around my softest places.

And all of it, I deserved through my courage. Through my decision to get to know the full-throttle Jesse.

Never before had I felt so transparent, like molten wax, a being ready to take on any form asked of me; and yet, so visible, so worshipped, as if I were made entirely of precious stones, meant only to be admired.

"Here's a tissue, big guy," I heard Jesse's voice from the next room, followed by Milan's enthusiastic "The strawberry one is the best!" and Bisera's swift rebuttal, "No, the caramel one," and then again Milan's "The strawberry one is the bestest!"

I made sure I was still wearing the T-shirt I'd thrown on earlier—the sheet alone wasn't secure enough with the kids liable to burst in at any moment—before shifting on the bed just enough to peer into the other room through the open doorway.

Milan and Bisera were attacking a tray of ice cream and waffles, their sticky little hands gleefully grabbing at the treats. Jesse caught me watching and smiled.

"Breakfast is served."

"You ordered ice cream for breakfast?" I raised an eyebrow.

"There are waffles too, Mama!" Milan chimed in, excitement bubbling in his voice.

"You mentioned ice cream yesterday at the beach," Jesse added with a grin.

I groaned and flopped back onto the pillow. He strolled in, sitting on the edge of the bed, his weight dipping the mattress. I could feel his eyes on me before I even saw them—warm, admiring, a little too knowing, reminding me of that thing unleashed between us with no slightest chance to cage it back in.

The good thing about being awake through one full sleep cycle was that it left no time to develop the usual morning puffiness or bad breath. Pushing my hair—which had soaked wet twice throughout the night—off my face I gave him a faint smile.

"Let's eat, then head out to the old town," he suggested, his warm palm resting on my ankle. "We can make it to St. Kaneo before the heat kicks in."

"What time is it?" I moaned.

"Eight."

"God, you're full of energy. You look like you slept more than two hours."

"I didn't sleep at all."

"You're kidding."

"Couldn't. So I went for a jog. It's amazing out there."

I stared at him, surprised. "You went for ... a jog?"

Was jogging his thing?

I imagined him running, mentally mapping out the best strategies for his clients, returning home with his restless mind tamed, chaotic thoughts neatly structured, ready to conquer the world. I couldn't help but wonder what kind of thoughts he was trying to organize after spending the night with me.

But instead, I asked, "How are you going to drive back home?"

"We'll see," he shrugged, unfazed. "So, what do you think? You in?"

"Damn," I muttered, sitting up, "I'd use the excuse that I didn't get enough sleep, but you didn't sleep at all, so I can't get away with it."

Jesse chuckled, his eyes locked on mine. His gaze had held so many things last night—hungry when he watched me go undone in his arms; adoring when the lights flicked back on and he insisted on keeping them that way; and finally, tender, just before I drifted off wrapped in his warmth. That same tenderness was there now, mingling with a grin that told me he hadn't stopped smiling since he sat beside me.

"If you don't want to go, we can stay here all day, hibernating like bears," he said.

"Let the kids destroy the room? No thanks," I shook my head. "Besides, I can't leave without climbing up to Kaneo."

"Okay then," he stood up. "Oh, by the way," Jesse added cautiously, "Milan has taken apart a couple of his toy cars. I brought him a screwdriver from the car. Only because he begged, not because I was curious how far he'd go."

I chuckled. "Yeah, he does that. He's got a natural curiosity for how things work. Either that or mechanical engineering. Both are fine by me."

"Thank God," Jesse laughed in guilty relief. "I was already bracing myself to put them back together."

"What, like it's hard for ya, Mr. Engineer?" I teased, pouting. He walked to my side of the bed, reaching for my hand and pulling me toward the edge. Straightening up on my knees, I faced him and wrapped my arms around his neck.

"If you do this," he murmured, his breath hot on my mouth, "I swear to god, I will find a babysitter who will take care of these kids, lock you in this room, and you won't see daylight for a week."

"I thought you liked watching them yourself," I replied, a playful challenge in my voice, trying to ignore his hands wandering over my ass. I already knew Jesse The Hoarder well enough, and I wasn't afraid of him. I would welcome him, again and again.

He slid one hand to my nape, taking a loose hold of my hair and tilting my head just enough to make me gasp. His mouth traced a slow line from my collarbone to my jaw.

"Right now," he said hoarsely, "some other instincts are taking over."

He kissed me with urgency, a demand we both recognized, the familiar path that would lead us exactly where we wanted, and quickly.

"Uncle Jesse!" Bisera's voice called from the other room, forcing us to break apart. "I think you should call a cleaning lady."

•　　　•　　　•

The kids hated walking around the town, but we stuck to our plan of going wherever we wanted and schlepping them along. We explored all of Old Town, poring over the street lamps shaped like traditional Ohrid houses, then the houses themselves, discussing why their second stories always extended over the narrow streets below. We bought hand-painted mugs for Betty and Nina—Harry Potter and Hermione Granger, meticulously crafted by local artists. We overtook groups of tourists, marveled at how cars managed to navigate the cramped streets, and imagined how common folk once strolled to the market, while rulers paraded through with their retinues, and invaders inevitably found themselves halted at the fortress on the hill.

We took pictures with the kids to send to Betty, lingered on a forest trail on our way to Kaneo in a slow kiss while kids were marvelling at snails. I caught Jesse's mischievous gaze as he said that the flush still lingering on my face from the previous night suited me (*"You should always look like this"*). We daydreamed aloud about one of those villas with its own dock and boat, even if it wasn't the prettiest or the newest of the boats, it would give us so much freedom to make our trips around the curve of the shore at any given moment.

"You already know what I'd name my boat," Jesse said.

I couldn't help but tease him. "Careful, it might not have the best fate."

He kissed my temple and replied, "But it'll be resilient."

We wrapped our trip up with lunch in a cafe perched on a cliff, offering a view of the entire town. From up here, it looked like the houses had been built in a haphazard order, their terracotta roofs scrambling for space as though each was trying to claim its own patch of sunlight. The hills surrounding Ohrid stood like silent sentinels, embracing the town in a protective circle, guarding it from whatever terrible things the world might send its way.

I stirred a spoon through the fig preserve that had been served as a welcome treat, waiting for our food. The kids were on the deck, leaning over the secure wooden railing, blowing soap bubbles we'd bought at the market. The bubbles floated lazily down the cliff, and the most persistent ones settled on rooftops far below.

"How did you and Stefan meet?" Jesse's voice pulled me back from my thoughts, his eyes shifting thoughtfully from the kids to meet mine.

Not that the question caught me off guard—I'd expected it at some point—but I had imagined it would come up under different circumstances, with a smoother lead-in, a mood that felt more prepared for it.

"Facebook," I replied, glancing away from him and down to the sweet sticky mass in my ramekin. "We got into a debate in the comments under some post about movies. I mentioned Tarantino and his ability to use the best cinematic traditions to bring his wildest fantasies to life, and Stefan started this whole thread about how Tarantino makes dumb movies." I smiled, looking up to the distant white clouds gathering like fragments of an unfinished story against the pale blue sky. "I tried to convince him that Tarantino's films are satire and ballsy intellectual roller coasters, but he wasn't having any of it. That same evening, he messaged me: 'If it weren't for your taste in movies, you'd be the perfect woman.'"

Jesse let out a low chuckle and nodded. "He was always bold."

"And direct," I added, the memory pulling at the corners of my lips. "I remember being furious and replying something like 'If you think that's bad, wait until you hear the rest of my opinions.' And somehow, instead of backing off, he doubled down. A week later, we were already video chatting. Two months after that, he flew me out here."

"And you stayed?"

"I came for a couple of weeks, but I kept pushing my return ticket back until he proposed. Around the same time, I found out I was pregnant."

I paused, letting the weight of those memories settle. The air around us felt still, as if it, too, was holding its breath. How long had it been since I'd let myself linger on those early days without the usual dull ache creeping in?

Jesse broke the silence, his voice softer. "When I saw you at the wedding back then, when you were in that lemon yellow dress, I thought ... well, a few things. The first was, how did this rascal manage to land someone like you?"

I laughed, meeting his gaze. He looked softer than I'd ever seen him, and that softness painted a disarming contrast against the tall, broad, and solid canvas of his being.

"I also noticed how happy Stefan looked," Jesse continued. "When we were friends, he was ... sullen. Moody. Careless. Mad. But at the wedding, he was someone I didn't recognize. Happy. I realized that was your doing."

Jesse's words hit like a soft blow, tender but piercing. I swallowed, feeling the sting of tears pushing at the corners of my eyes. It was an odd thing—having someone tell you something you already knew, but not letting yourself believe it until it was reflected back to you in someone else's voice.

"And you," he added, "you were glowing. Radiating warmth. But when I saw you again at 'Tuscany,' it was like that glow had faded. There was this guarded, restrained energy around you. Pain." His brow furrowed slightly with a small shake of his head. "It wasn't how I remembered you. And I felt this strong urge to check on you, to see if you needed help, or if something was wrong. But then, sitting in your home with Lazar, it wasn't hard to figure out what had caused that change. Beyond losing Stefan, I mean."

I nodded, pressing my lips together. His words stretched to me like an invisible hand gripping my heart. "Sometimes it feels like they're draining the life out of me," I said without looking at him. "When Stefan was around, the dynamic was different." There was so much more I wasn't saying—couldn't say. The thought of burdening him with my family issues more than I already had, and doing it here, at this magical place he brought me to, felt unfair. Yet somehow, Jesse understood, and I saw the muscle in his jaw tighten.

His voice was lighter when he said, "But now ... I see that glow again."

I blinked, caught off guard.

He beamed at my surprise. "I'm not trying to take credit for it. It's this place. You feel good here. And it's far away from everything you're forced to deal with."

My eyes hooked with his, a faint smile pulling at my lips. "I think you should take some credit for it."

His eyes lingered on mine, a quiet warmth replacing the guarded look he'd worn moments ago. Before I could follow that thought, the sound of Milan and Bisera's excited squeals floated across the terrace.

"Look!" Milan's voice was full of wonder, pulling my attention. The two of them were huddled by a corner of the room, mesmerized by the goldfish swimming in loops in an aquarium. Their little fingers were pressed to the glass, eyes wide with fascination.

We both turned, watching them with a kind of quiet comfort. The small round table between us felt more like a bridge than a gap—comfortable, offering space for thoughts we might otherwise hesitate to share.

"Were you really engaged?" I asked, thinking of the quasi-casual comment Betty threw in the air when we were eating pancakes at his place.

Jesse paused, considering the question. "Yeah."

"Will you tell me about it?"

He glanced at the scenery spreading before us, perhaps gathering his thoughts. "We met in Dubai. She worked at the same firm as me. Six months later, we were engaged. Another six months and we broke it off."

"What happened?"

He hesitated before answering, his voice more distant now. "She told her family."

I tried to make a teasing comment thinking I was as far from the real reason as one could possibly be. "What, her dad didn't approve?"

A faint smile played on his lips but didn't quite reach his eyes. "Her mom."

"God." I winced inwardly at my flippancy. "Are you for real?" and then added, pointing somewhere between his sculptured jawline and his bicep prominent through the white T-shirt, "Did she even see you?"

He let out a dry chuckle, shaking his head. "If only Macedonian parents—or any parents for that matter—made decisions based on looks."

"Man! And here I was thinking my mother-in-law approved of me because of my fine curves."

That earned a real laugh, his eyes softening as he looked at me in a way that could've melted me right there if I let it.

"These things happen here," Jesse said. "You might be surprised, but Stefan's family is probably more open-minded since they accepted a foreigner—especially one as strong-willed as you. It's not to say they are with the most modern views, obviously, but there are more conservative families in this country."

"Still, I like to think Vesna simply grew to love me. She still does, even though I've been ... difficult."

"I'm sure she does love you. You are very much like Stefan's father. Stubborn, loud, and funny."

I froze for a moment, my gaze snapping back to him. Stefan had always said his father would have loved me, that we were kindred spirits, but I'd chalked it up to wishful thinking.

"You knew him?" I asked, my throat tightening.

"Of course," Jesse replied, leaning forward. "I spent a lot of time in that house. We'd hang out in the unfinished rooms on the second floor, listening to music and playing cards, Vesna bringing sandwiches and Gazoza; Oliver washing his car in the yard, cracking jokes with the neighbors, his laughter echoing through the street."

"Wow." The vivid image of those days came together in my mind like pieces of a puzzle I never knew existed.

"Ilaria," he called, bringing my eyes back on him. "I spent my whole adolescence being Stefan's friend. And even though we drifted apart later ... it feels unreal not to have him around in this town. I miss him, too."

It was fortunate that the waiter swung by, unloading our order dish by dish onto the table. I was on the brink of tears, dangerously close to breaking my own promise not to ruin the day with crying. While the waiter momentarily blocked Jesse's view of me, I took a few deep breaths and called out to the kids, who were still busy harassing the goldfish. They came running back to the table, eyeing the food like little vultures. It was almost noon, and their last meal had been the waffle-ice-cream disaster at 8 a.m., so I didn't need to put my ear to their little stomachs to know they were growling. But I sent them to wash their hands first. They mumbled protests, dragging their feet reluctantly toward the restroom as the waiter showed them the way.

"So," I said, still wanting to know the rest of Jesse's story, "her family didn't approve of you ... why?"

He shrugged, lifting the napkin off his plate and setting it aside. "Maybe they didn't like my family. Or my lifestyle. I was always traveling, and they wanted her to have a stable life at home. They wanted her to settle down with kids."

"And what did *she* want?"

"I think it was easier for her not to go home and deal with it. We kept things as they were for a while, but eventually ... it just faded. Not because we couldn't have gotten married, but because she wasn't sure her parents were wrong."

I felt a pang in my chest. Jesse and I had more in common than I'd realized.

We were both shaped by the weight of others' opinions—how reputations and expectations had nudged us into paths we hadn't necessarily chosen. When he'd spoken of resilience earlier, I hadn't fully grasped it. But now, I saw it clearly in him. Jesse had borne all of it—every judgment, every slight—without a shred of bitterness. No resentment lingered in his words.

That was a bigger generosity than I could offer. The woman agreed to marry him, but gave him up because of prejudice of people she didn't even want to live next to since she'd chosen to escape to Dubai. If I were him, I would have a hole the size of a plane hangar in my chest.

"I don't harbour ill feelings against them," Jesse said as if reading it all in my face. "They just have a certain way of thinking. You can't expect people to generate behaviour that's not in their DNA. It's like ... When I lived in Japan, I could never expect people to openly express their emotions, because it's not in their mentality. So, if I had tried to change that, I would have faced disappointment over and over again."

"But then ... how do you find a place where you belong?"

"I don't know," he pursed his lips. "I guess I just don't."

"You will leave again, won't you?" I asked, my voice barely above a whisper. I hadn't meant it to sound so vulnerable, so exposed. But the question was there, and it lingered between us.

I noticed a sudden shift in his eyes, a new, pale expression settling in—heavy and core-shaking, as if he were wrestling with something vital, something life-altering. Yet there was a flicker of something raw and fragile just beneath the surface. It made my heart ache, though I couldn't fully grasp why.

"What is it?" I asked.

Jesse sighed, a soft exhale that seemed to carry the weight of unspoken things. He stretched out his hand, and I took it without hesitation. He gently moved from his chair to the loveseat, the one meant for Bisera and Milan, and pulled me into his arms. That familiar scent of his—cedary and sunny—triggered something deep within me, ringing through my bones and settling into the very essence of me, like it belonged there.

He held me tighter than usual, and I knew it had something to do with that sudden realization of his, but I didn't ask anything. I just nestled into his neck, letting myself simply *be* once again this weekend.

Milan came bursting back from the restroom, all energy and bright eyes. He clambered into my chair like he owned it, and before I could even react, Bisera flopped down in Jesse's seat, her tiny hands still dripping from the wash-up.

They both tore into the pita with their little pearly teeth, their minds fixed on the here and now, focused solely on the pieces of dough, chicken, and melted cheese. They weren't thinking about tomorrow; they'd already forgotten about the goldfish and the soap bubbles. Once again, I found myself envying that childlike ability to be present, without complicating things, without drifting into the past or future.

Obviously, we decided to stay for one more night.

Because Jesse hadn't slept and was in no condition to drive.

Because the day had slipped by too quickly. Because the thought of leaving lit a cold fire in my stomach that I didn't want to confront yet. I wanted to stay a little longer, daydreaming about our own villa and a boat with my name painted on it. I wanted to count, categorize and label every one of his glances. I wanted to spend another night surrounded by his scent, wrapped in the strength of his arms.

Because, though I couldn't quite put it into words, I had the sense that this ... this might be all we would ever get.

8

I HADN'T BEEN to a wedding in ages.

Someone in my circle of friends and relatives seemed to get married every other month, with at least five weddings a year. But I'd turned down every invitation since Stefan's death. Widowhood gave me an easy out, and no one pressed me too hard—it was common knowledge that widows cast a shadow over such celebrations. Even if they did show up, they weren't expected to laugh or dance. Not that I had any desire to.

Social gatherings had never been easy for me anyway—the only real draw was being out with my husband. Hearing the familiar voice next to me in a room full of strangers; the anticipation of his reaction when I had a joke or an observation to share; knowing where exactly I will find his hand if I reach for it.

All that, and dancing. I had come to find a strange, almost tribal allure in oro, that intricate circle dance. Moving in unison, step after step, the quiet satisfaction when the rhythm held and no one faltered felt like an ancient pulse in my veins, a connection to something far older. But for an entire year, I had made my body remain silent. It was only now that I realized how fiercely I had closed myself off to any pleasure, however small. Joy and grief couldn't coexist.

How strange, then, that tradition had worked its way into my life with such eerie precision. I had been given a year of mourning, according to all the old customs. I had never taken such ossified traditions seriously—rituals whose origins no one remembered, whose reasons no one could explain. How could anyone know how long grief should last? Psychology would say I might've been ready to return to life after six months, or I might still be crying myself to sleep two years from now. There were no rules.

But here was the irony: I met Jesse one year and two months after Stefan's death. As if the universe itself was mocking me. *So, you don't take tradition seriously? Here you go, proof of its power.*

Looking back, I think Jesse became my gentle alarm clock, waking me from a sleep that had gone on too long. Life sometimes does that—nudges you forward. First gently, with hints and whispers, and if you don't listen, it starts throwing boulders.

I got the hint. I took his hand and let my body wake up again.

I'm not sure I would have come to this wedding if I hadn't met him, hadn't started to feel the pull of life in my lungs again. In all likelihood, I wouldn't have come at all if I didn't know he'd be there. Because no matter how ready I was to start participating in life's celebrations, the thought of sitting at a table with Danche and Lazar was enough to cancel out any joy the occasion might promise.

Not that I expected much from his presence. We wouldn't sit together, we wouldn't share a dance, and we'd barely get to exchange a few words. But just knowing he would be there made the three hours in the company of people who would likely glance at me with either pity or prying curiosity seem somewhat bearable.

So maybe I hadn't fully recovered after all. Perhaps I still hated people. *Should I even go?*

I seriously considered that question as I stood in front of the mirror, choosing earrings. Vesna, already dressed in her green slacks and a new black-and-white blouse, was strutting up and down the hallway, testing her heels. I stepped aside to give her the mirror, complimenting her outfit and the hairstyle the neighbor, a hairdresser, had pulled together for her earlier.

Vesna looked every bit like a woman in her early seventies who had kept her fair hair meticulously styled. Her sharp features immediately explained which parent her sons took after, though age had softened her face into a kind of dignity.

"Have you decided what you're wearing yet?" she asked.

Knowing we'd cross paths in front of this mirror, I had deliberately avoided putting on my dress. Vesna, like every Macedonian mother-in-law and grandmother, lived for her family, driven by a firm belief that she was unconditionally needed by her children and grandchildren. Her attention, hovering and unsolicited, left no room for anyone to dismiss her. I understood her, but I had no intention of indulging her. Not out of principle, but because it had taken me some time to realize something about myself since joining this family—I suffocated under the constant, intrusive closeness, the lack of an escape. But because I was grateful to Vesna for all her help and support, I had developed my own coping mechanisms. Instead of hearing how this dress "didn't suit me" or how I should wear "the other one," and instead of risking being rude or hurt, I simply waited until she was gone to get dressed.

"I haven't decided yet," I answered, fastening a long gold earring. From the bathroom came Milan's singsong voice, humming a melody.

"Lazar said he could drive you," Vesna offered, meeting my gaze in the mirror.

"Won't his car be full?"

"I'm riding with Aunt Marta, and Danche has taken the kids to her mother's, so ... there's plenty of room in their car."

I reached for the second earring, weighing the prospect of ten minutes of awkward silence that sharing a ride with those two would entail.

"I'll take a taxi."

I think Vesna knew I'd say that, but she never gave up on trying to mend the rift between her sons, to bring the family together, to make us all stick to each other in this big, cruel world, despite our differences. Even though she hadn't spoken to her own brother in years—but that was different.

When Aunt Marta called to say she was waiting outside, and Vesna made her slow exit, I glanced out the window: Lazar's car was still there. For some reason, I wanted to wait until they were gone before I ordered a taxi. I was about to step out into the world for the first time in a long while, and I felt a slippery, cold knot in my stomach—the feeling that I'd be too easy to read if I bumped into them on the driveway, as though everything would be written on my face, that the past two weeks with Jesse had stripped away too many layers, leaving me without the armor I usually relied on.

As if just one look at me would be enough for them to know what happened in Ohrid. That the day after we returned, the moment I dropped Milan off at daycare, I was at Jesse's place, back in his arms. And later, he made French toast. When I offered to help, he smiled and said my hands already had one burn too many, but I could handle the cold coffee if I was so eager to participate. And within minutes, we were making love again in his kitchen.

It feels like my face says it all—that I've spent every morning of this week at his place. And whenever I'd ask if he needed to go to work, he'd just shrug, saying there was nothing urgent that couldn't wait until the afternoon, even though his phone would ring or beep persistently, which he nonchalantly ignored until he just muted it.

It's as if, just by looking at me, it's obvious that last night, we had dinner with Betty and her entire family at Jesse's house. The older kids played for nearly four hours straight, we took turns holding baby Adam until he fell asleep in his father's ams, talked about simple things, joked shamelessly, laughed indecently, and I was so blissfully content that it felt like the kind of happiness you don't even speak of aloud.

And today—this wedding. We'll have to pretend like none of it ever happened. I wasn't even sure anymore which part of my life felt more surreal, and which was truly mine.

From the bathroom came the sound of a flush, and I asked Milan if everything was alright, to which he replied with a cheerful hum and the splash of the tap water. I folded white socks to go with his olive cotton shorts and short-sleeved shirt draped over the chair, then moved to the closet.

Yes, I'd told Vesna I hadn't decided what to wear yet. But when I'd braided my hair into a half halo, loose and casual, letting the rest fall in boho waves; when I'd thought of the only person I truly wanted to see tonight; and when I turned over in my mind all the things I wanted to say to him, even though we'd barely have a chance to exchange more than a few words—I knew exactly what dress I wanted to wear.

·　　　·　　　·

Judging by the buzz echoing from the banquet hall, Milan and I were among the last guests to arrive. The bride and groom—weariness carefully masked by thrilled expressions, as their day had likely begun at dawn—were posing by the photo backdrop with a family who'd arrived just minutes before us. The air greeted us with a complex blend of perfumes, each guest adding their own note to the heady mix.

I'd never been to this hotel before, but the grand staircase leading up to the restaurant was impossible to miss. As we made our way toward it, I caught sight of a small group of men standing on the upper step, deep in conversation just outside the entrance. My heart gave a faint, unexpected jolt, the sensation rippling through my stomach.

Jesse was one of them. Tall and angular, his dark hair tousled just enough to make him look effortlessly attractive. His broad shoulders filled out the sharp lines of his tailored suit, the midnight-blue fabric catching just enough light to emphasize his frame.

He noticed me mid-sentence, his words halting as his gaze locked on me. For one-two-three heartbeats, he just stared, lips parted. The conversation around him seemed to pause as his companions glanced in the same direction, following his gaze. I knew what they saw—another elegant guest in the silk-manicure-makeup camouflage. Dozens had likely glided through those doors in the past hour.

But I knew what Jesse saw—the lemon-colored dress. His eyes traced the thin spaghetti straps, then slowly traveled down the fabric that hugged my waist and flared gently over my hips, cascading just above my heels.

I wondered if, at that moment—when his eyes filled with awe and recognition—he was comparing the faded, distant image worn down by time to this new version of me, the one he could actually reach out and touch.

For a fleeting moment, the urge to walk straight over to him, take his hand, and disappear was almost overwhelming. But something about tonight felt like a challenge—to see if I could make it through the evening without falling back into the comfort of his presence, without relying on the steady anchor he'd become far too quickly.

The family in front of us finished their photos, and soon it was our turn. Milan ran ahead to greet the happy couple, and I followed, exchanging pleasantries with the bride in her elaborate beaded gown and the tall, slender groom in his tuxedo. I suddenly remembered that the groom, Sasha, had once been Betty's boyfriend. I suppose it was an odd thing to acknowledge on his wedding day, but I'd only known Betty for so long. Seeing her yesterday with her husband and two sweet kids made me marvel at the strange, unpredictable paths life takes to give us something *good*. If Betty and Sasha had never fallen out, would she be standing next to him now? Would they have been having dinner with us yesterday, radiating that messy-but-happy family vibe all along?

We smiled for the camera, standing against the backdrop of a white and pink floral arch, our faces lit with polite excitement.

Once we finished, I climbed the stairs, my heels tapping softly against the marble. Jesse stood alone now, his smile tight, strained—as though he were caught between enduring small talk and wanting to be anywhere but here. Milan raced ahead, slapping Jesse's outstretched palm in a boisterous high-five before disappearing into the crowd.

Jesse stepped back, allowing me to pass, his expression defeated. I knew he followed me inside, falling into step just close enough that I could sense him without looking, even through the grumble of Balkan instruments that reigned over the spacious hall.

His voice, hoarse and low, came close to my ear, "That felt like a sucker punch."

I smirked, craning my head toward him, unable to resist the tease. "I thought you liked it a little rough."

He let out a low, throaty growl, and I remembered how he made the same exact sound yesterday into the curve of my neck when we were rolling in his bed, right before we realized the neighbor's cat had just witnessed the entire show through the window.

The two realities I was a part of, somehow merged into one right there, in that restaurant, and it felt like the quantum continuum gave a crack.

Jesse offered me one last glance, his eyes dark with amusement, before shaking his head and veering toward the opposite side of the hall, away from where I was seated.

9

"WHITE OR RED?" the waiter asked as I glanced at the bottles placed in the very center of our round table. The appetizers were already there, too, and the waitstaff fluttered around, eager to fill glasses before the bride and groom made their grand entrance, kicking off the evening's rituals.

"White, please," I said, noticing that Lazar, Danche, and Vesna already had their rakija glasses filled. Aunt Marta and her grown daughter, Vaska, gave a knowing look as the waiter poured white wine into my glass—both of theirs already shimmered with the same.

Of course, I expected no other outcome than sitting with Stefan's family. Wedding planners don't really care if you get along with your relatives—they just shove the clans together like it's some kind of mandatory survival exercise. But I hoped to spend most of the evening on my feet—dancing the oro or chasing after Milan, who would inevitably find some adventure to throw himself into.

"Where's Milan?" Vesna asked.

I scanned the room, a weird maze of randomly placed columns. "Somewhere here. He was just running with two kids from that table."

"Gordana's grandkids," Vesna offered. She did that often—effortlessly tossed out names of people I barely knew. At least this time, she had an audience in Aunt Marta, who would eagerly dissect who Gordana was—her husband, her daughter-in-law, her job, and, most importantly, her reputation—to stir up the familiar satisfaction of shared recognition.

Jesse was seated at the other end of the hall, within my line of sight, and he occasionally threw me brief glances in between conversations with his tablemates. Lucky him, he wasn't stuck with family—just another "single guest" seated with random couples or fellow loners.

Suddenly, I spotted a small figure in a white shirt and olive shorts making a beeline for Jesse. Milan tugged at his sleeve, and my stomach twisted.

My son, who wasn't supposed to know Jesse all that well, trusted him enough to climb into his arms. Jesse hoisted Milan effortlessly, carrying him across the restaurant, weaving around the guitarist and waiter with a big-ass tray—right toward me.

Under the curious stares of Stefan's family, which quickly morphed into enthusiastic greetings, Jesse set Milan down beside me and greeted everyone as though he'd been born into this wedding. The way Aunt Marta asked, "How are you, Jesse?" made it obvious there was no need to introduce him to anyone here.

"This big guy got lost and couldn't find his mom," Jesse said, looking at me with zero awkwardness—as if we were just casual acquaintances. "So, I decided to escort him to your table."

I can do it, I can mimic his nonchalant attitude. The fact that my hips had been wrapped around his just ten hours ago doesn't have to dictate the way I feel, the way I act or whether or not I flush.

Vesna's eyes darted between Milan and Jesse in the increasingly stifling air, so I rushed to clarify.

"Jesse has a niece, and Milan's obsessed with her."

"Seems mutual," Jesse added, locking his gaze with mine just for half a beat, a hidden smile playing at the corners of his eyes and disappearing as soon as he returned his eyes to the intrigued "crowd".

"They go to the same daycare?" Danche chimed in, her voice oddly out of place. I turned to her, mentally rewinding the last few seconds like stepping on scattered stones to cross a river, trying to figure out how we got here.

"No," Jesse cut in smoothly, "They met recently at the playground and now insist on seeing each other every chance they get."

Milan, clutching the back of my chair, added proudly, "Bisera's got a big black Jeep with four-wheel drive."

"A future daughter-in-law, then," Vesna teased, flashing a sly grin, and we all laughed, steering the conversation toward lighter waters.

Jesse excused himself, reminding us that the bride and groom would make their entrance any moment now—a perfectly timed excuse to divert my attention to the center of the room rather than risk catching too-interested glances from my in-laws.

As Jesse strode back to his seat, Milan tugged at my sleeve, his curiosity apparently awakened. "Why isn't Jesse sitting with us?"

Panic surged through me. Of course, Milan, with his innocent straightforwardness, couldn't know that dropping Jesse's name too casually in this crowd was the verbal equivalent of tossing a live grenade into the middle of the table. If they pressed him on why he thought Jesse *should* be here with us—he would most probably blurt out something about how we've all been spending time together—and not exactly at the playground.

"Oh, uh, well ..." I glanced quickly at Vesna and the others, feeling my palms go cold as I tried to think fast. "You see, Milan, Jesse's sitting over there because, um, he's making sure that if you get lost again, he can help guide you back to our table."

Milan nodded, wide-eyed with understanding, and I felt a small surge of relief, thankful he bought it. "So I can see him from anywhere and come to him?"

"Exactly!" I said, managing not to wince at how easily I'd dodged the bullet. I kept my eyes fixed firmly ahead, pretending to be deeply invested in not missing the grand entrance of the bride and groom—who, as far as I was concerned, could take all the time in the world.

But within two minutes, the bride and groom glided onto the dance floor for their first dance, the hall showering them with applause and celebratory screams.

After another four minutes, the slow strains of the next song followed, an invitation for all the couples to join. I felt Danche and Lazar standing up to head to the center of the room as I eyed my own fingers tracing the strap of my purse on my lap and bracing to sit another love song out.

But when I raised my eyes, Jesse was already halfway across the room, moving toward me with that same casual grace. He stopped by a column, just far enough to be discreet, but close enough that I knew what he was offering.

I couldn't help but laugh under my breath. Even from across a crowded room, Jesse had a way of pulling me in like a force of nature. The kind that could cause chaos or calm, depending on the moment.

"Well, someone's bold tonight," I muttered, when I met him halfway.

And there was a familiar flicker of mischief in his eyes when he held out his hand. "Bold? I'm just following the wedding protocol. You know, dancing with a guest in need."

I raised a brow, letting his fingers curl around mine as we slipped away from the crowded tables. "That's what this is? Protocol?"

"Oh, absolutely," he deadpanned. "I take these things very seriously. I'm practically a wedding expert at this point."

A laugh slipped out before I could stop it, and he grinned—satisfied.

As we moved into the soft glow of the dance floor, the reality of it all hit me: I was in Jesse's arms in front of two hundred people. His hand settled at the small of my back, and the gentle weight of it was enough to send a shiver through me. His touch, though perfectly respectable, still felt electric, like a reminder of the things we weren't allowed to express here. My heart raced, and suddenly, it was hard to focus on anything other than the warmth of his palm through the thin fabric of my dress.

He smelled like cedarwood and rain, the same scent that clung to every item of my clothes he'd touched. I could feel the memory flooding back—his hands on my hips, his mouth drinking up my ragged gasps, the heat of his skin sliding against mine—and now here we were, pretending to be nothing more than casual friends on a crowded dance floor. The contrast was maddening, almost laughable.

I wanted to sink into him, feel the safety and solidity of his chest pressed to mine like it had been when no one else was watching. But we weren't alone now, and the weight of unseen eyes pressed heavily on me. I could almost feel the judgment circling, the whispers waiting to ignite the moment we stepped away.

But then his thumb brushed the bare skin of my back— deliberate, slow, just barely enough to notice. I looked up, catching his gaze as he turned us slowly in time to the music. His eyes, dark and intent, were locked on me with that same intensity they always held in private, like he could see straight through me.

I bit my lip, trying not to get lost in that look. How was he so composed, so maddeningly calm, while every part of me felt like it was burning from the inside out? His clean-shaved jaw was tense, but his expression didn't betray much else—just the slightest quirk of his lips when he watched me chew onto my lower lip.

"You're trouble," he murmured, low enough for only me to hear.

I shot my eyebrows in surprise, "Me? Why?"

"You look like you're ready to take off with me right now."

I laughed quietly, almost dropping my head on his chest, but straightened up immediately, rolling my shoulders back and clearing my throat.

"I was ready long before I came here," I replied still smiling at him.

His eyes danced over my face as he said, "That cheeky grin of yours is going to give us away."

Oh, they'd talk regardless. I could already feel the stares from Lazar and Danche who were spinning a few feet away. A widow, dancing with another man at a family event—how scandalous.

But it wasn't just the public aspect that made this feel reckless. There was a primal part of me that ached to be claimed, to kiss him out in the open, to make it known that I was his and he was mine. It was irrational, wild, and entirely impractical given the tangled mess that was my life. And yet, it flickered inside me, urging me forward.

I wondered if Jesse felt it too, that pull to declare what we had, to stop pretending. Men had that instinct, didn't they? To stake a claim, to make it known to the world. Part of me craved that—an unapologetic, public display. To kiss him at a coffee shop, step out of his car in the city center, hold hands at concerts. To just *be* happy with him, no secrets.

But could I? With everything hanging over me—my in-laws, Milan, Stefan's memory—it felt like something I wasn't sure I had the right to want. I sighed, leaning my head just a fraction closer, savoring the moment while it lasted. Jesse's fingers tightened, just slightly, around mine, as though he could sense the internal battle raging inside me.

"Everything alright?" he whispered, his breath hot against my ear which meant he was entirely too close, but I couldn't make myself pull back or let him. I thought I would fall into pieces if he did.

So I just nodded. If anything in my life was alright, it was this. It's the outside of it that was a caustic disappointment.

.   .   .

I barely make it back to my seat before the weight of the evening slams into me. I can feel their eyes—Lazar's first, burning into me from across the table. Danche tries to say something, but she's too quiet, and Lazar's voice slices through the moment like a cold wind.

"Could you at least not do it at a family function?"

I look down at him, heart pounding. "Not do what?"

"You know exactly what."

I grip the back of my chair, his words cutting deeper than they should, and I'm still standing near my seat as five pairs of eyes are pinning me expecting me to crumble. But I won't give them that satisfaction. I meet Lazar's gaze, steady and cold. "I didn't think I needed your permission."

Lazar's jaw clenches, his nostrils flaring. "This all is disrespectful to Stefan."

And that's when it hits me—this isn't about me, or the dance, or the wedding. It's about him, his need to control, to pull me back under. I can feel the anger rise, simmering just below the surface, hot and fierce.

"That's rich coming from you," I say, my voice low, each word measured. "You didn't respect him when he was alive. Now you want to *start* respecting him?"

His chair scrapes harshly against the floor as he stands, towering over me. The air between us thickens with unspoken threats. "Watch your mouth."

Danche's hand shoots up to his arm, her face pale, pleading. "Not here, Lazar."

I know she hates public arguments more than anything. They make you lose your well-reputed face and give people the reason for tea.

But Lazar is not listening to his spouse. As calculated as he's always been, he is also short-tempered. His eyes are locked on me, full of judgment and indignation. The rest of the room could be watching, or no one at all—I can't tell anymore. It's just him, his anger, and mine crashing against each other.

"You're embarrassing us," he spits out, like he's tearing pieces of me down with every syllable.

Embarrassing them. Always them. As if my life should revolve around not making them uncomfortable. My skin prickles with heat, my pulse racing. "If I'm embarrassing you," I say, voice sharp, "maybe you should let me sell my part of the ground so that I can be out of your sight."

His mouth twists, eyes narrowing with contempt. "I will make sure you never see an inch of that land," and then he adds, "What kind of mother are you? Your son is right here!"

A shadow passes behind me, and before I can fully register it, Jesse's voice cuts through the tension like a lifeline.

"Enough."

I don't turn. I don't need to. I can feel him, steady and calm, standing just behind me. His presence washes over me like a wave of cool air. Lazar's anger is hot, suffocating, but Jesse is something else entirely—solid, unwavering. And though my hands are still trembling, the storm inside me still raging, his calm centers me.

Lazar's eyes dart from me to Jesse, his face a mess of frustration and bitterness. "It's a family matter, stay out of it," he snaps.

But Jesse doesn't flinch, doesn't even raise his voice. "You're making a scene in the middle of your family member's wedding."

Lazar stiffens, his chest rising and falling too fast. "It's none of your damn business, Jesse."

Jesse steps forward, close enough now that I can feel the fabric of his shirt against my bare shoulders. His voice is low, firm, but there's something else in it, something deeper. Protective. "We're done here, Lazar. If you think you can take this further, look me in the eye and think again."

Lazar's mouth opens, but no words come out. The silence that follows is heavy, choking. I can see the rage boiling beneath his skin, but something in Jesse's tone—something in his stance—makes him hesitate. Makes him stop.

I catch Lazar's eyes flicker with uncertainty. There's fear there too, barely noticeable, but I see it. And another squeeze of Danche's hand on his makes him step back and slam on his chair.

It's too much. All of it. The fight, the tension, Jesse standing there like a shield between me and this mess of a family. I excuse myself—no idea to whom in particular—and rush across the hall towards the exit.

·   ·   ·

And when Jesse finds me in the alcove, I'm still trying to get a grip on everything that just happened. It's like I'm caught between wanting to disappear into the cold stone wall behind me and the sudden warmth that floods the space when he steps closer. I hear his footsteps first, slow and steady, and though I know it's him, my body tenses.

He's here, and somehow that makes it all real—the fight, the whispers, the weight of everything I've been holding back.

When he stands near me, he doesn't say anything right away, and I don't need him to. The silence between us is thick but comforting, a space where I can exist without having to pretend. But then he says my name, and I feel like something inside me breaks. I can't look at him at first; I'm too wrapped up in my own mess, the embarrassment, the anger, the regret. But I don't want to be alone. Not now.

And when I finally meet his eyes, the concern in them undoes me. I can tell Jesse is hesitating; he's still figuring out when I need to be held and when I need to stand on my own. But right now, all I want is to collapse into him.

When he says, "You don't have to tolerate any of this," it's like he's speaking to a part of me that I've been trying to silence for years. I know he's right, but knowing and doing are two very different things.

And when he holds me closer, wrapping his arms around me *like I am his*, I feel it all come crashing down. The anger, the humiliation, the guilt—it all bubbles to the surface, threatening to spill over. But in his arms, it feels safer to unravel, like I won't drown if I let the tears fall. I don't have to hold it all together anymore, at least not at that moment. He isn't asking me to.

And then he says he's going to take me home, and something about the way he says it—so soft, so certain—makes 'home' feel different. Like it's not just a place, but a promise. I know he means his house, but he's offering it to me as a safe harbor. So when I nod and lean into him, it's not just because I'm tired or broken or lost. It's because I know, in this moment, that wherever he is— that's where I want to be.

10

I SPENT THE NIGHT AT JESSE'S, clutching my son in my arms like some kind of shield against the mess I'd created. Had I ruined everything for Milan? What would his relationship with Lazar, Danche, and their kids—people he'd grown up with—look like from now on? If they truly decided they never wanted to see us again, what could I possibly give him, all on my own? He's already lost someone who was his best friend, who gave him everything, more than any other father I saw giving, who was there for him in every possible way. Can I really replace everything that Stefan used to be for him? Can I fill that gaping hole in my boy's chest once the noise and chaos of a big family dies down, and it's just the two of us?

There was a time I worried Lazar's family would influence him in the wrong way, teach him that "social lie" skill, that duplicity they wield so expertly. Now I was worried they wouldn't, and he would end up not fitting in—just like his mom.

Jesse, who had slept in another room, peeked in the morning to whisper in my ear that he was heading out to show the vineyards to a potential buyer and would be back in an hour.

He returned with coffee, hot chocolate, and a slice of tres leches cake just as Milan and I had already freshened up using the spare toothbrushes and whipped up scrambled eggs for all of us. I met him in the doorway with a silicone spatula in my hand, my half-halo braid falling apart, leaving my hair looking like some untamed horse's mane, and underneath an apron (which I hadn't expected to find in a man cave) peeked my yellow silk dress. Jesse grinned and handed me a bag. Inside were a t-shirt and shorts, and he explained it was so I "wouldn't have to go back home in that same dress with the neighbours watching."

If I knew how to thank him properly, aside from the eggs, I would've done it, but he seemed completely content, as if he already had everything he needed. So I changed into the comfortable clothes, marveling at how perfectly he guessed my size, and we sat down to breakfast, with Jesse casually mentioning that the buyer was ready to sign the deal on Monday, while he and Milan discussed the horsepower of Japanese cars.

After breakfast, though, Jesse's calm started to waver—tiny flickers of tension: a thoughtful glance lasting a fraction too long, his hand grazing his chin, teeth worrying at his lower lip. And as soon as I sent Milan off to watch his 30 minutes of cartoons—his hard-earned screen time—Jesse finally spoke. And oh god, I wish I could've undone it right there, rewound time, and returned to the blissful ignorance of a minute ago.

"I called Lazar," he said, catching me by the wrist as I started to rise to clear the table. I froze, sat back down, eyes locked on him, unblinking.

He continued, "I offered Danche a job with our firm in exchange for Lazar leaving you alone and agreeing to split the property that's rightfully yours."

"You did … what?!"

My voice cracked through the room like a whip, eyes widening in disbelief. The words hung in the air for a beat, like they didn't quite belong in this reality.

Jesse's tone was maddeningly steady as he began explaining himself.

"As I said I couldn't secure a contract with Lazar. But we've been looking for a billing specialist, and that's Danche's field of expertise. The pay is one and a half times the average market rate, and she won't have to commute. They agreed immediately. They'll probably be very nice to you from now on."

I stared at him, completely incredulous.

"Why ... why did you do that?"

The words were soft at first, then gained strength as the anger brewed. "Oh my god, Jesse! *They will be nice to me?* They've always been nice to me! That's never been the problem!"

"But I thought ... " He faltered for a moment, but before he could finish, I was up, my chair scraping loudly against the parquet floor.

"Do you think I've been hating their guts because they weren't nice to me?"

I was pacing now, hands flying up in exasperation. "No! I hate them because they're fake! Their niceness is bullshit! They smile in your face, pretend to care, but it's all an act. They think they're entitled to my respect just because they're masters at pretending! And now—now they'll try even harder to hide how much they hate me because you've just gifted them a damn job!"

Jesse remained unnervingly calm, his brown eyes boring into mine, as if searching for something deeper beneath my frustration. His voice dropped an octave, laced with a quiet intensity that contrasted with my spiraling.

"Why do you care whether they really like you or not? Isn't it enough if they just treat you with respect?"

I paused mid-step, my breath catching in my throat. His words echoed in the space between us, challenging me in ways I hadn't expected.

"Because I hate games, Jesse. I hate murky, twisted relationships where nothing is clear. I want honesty! I can't stand being surrounded by fake smiles. You can't be yourself around people like that. You can't trust them."

He nodded slightly, his gaze even more penetrating.

"Okay, I get that." He paused, his voice calm but serious. "So, just sell the land and go. You'll have enough to buy a house or an apartment, and you won't have to be around them anymore."

I rubbed the bridge of my nose, trying to process everything. The idea of leaving, cutting ties—it seemed like such an easy solution. Yet, it felt impossibly heavy. And then an understanding settled in my mind, like I finally saw the sky—clear and cloudless: he had just committed an act of nepotism. For me. For my sake. So that I could get the fucking justice.

I turned toward him, my brow furrowed.

"Did you even check her background? Did you ask her about her experience?"

Jesse blinked, confused.

"What?"

"Danche," I snapped, my voice rising. "How do you even know she's qualified for the job?"

"She worked at 'Aktiva' for years in the same position. I'm sure she's good enough."

I scoffed, shaking my head.

"You compromised your integrity for this deal. They don't deserve it. I have a right to that land. And with this—this bribe—you've made them think I don't. I'd rather rent some shitty flat in the city center, with motorbikes screaming past my window and live music shaking the walls until one in the morning, than let you negotiate anything with them!"

Jesse's sigh was almost inaudible. "I bet you didn't think that when you first met them."

I stopped, my gaze snapping to his.

"I bet when you first came here, you were the most open, accepting person in the world." Jesse continued, his voice steady, yet there was an undercurrent of something deeper, something raw. "You probably looked for the reasons behind people's behaviour, didn't you? Not judging them right away. I blame Stefan for what he's put you through."

His words landed like a punch to the gut. I took a step back, my throat tightening.

And you, you were glowing. Radiating warmth. But when I saw you again at 'Tuscany,' it was like that glow had faded.

"Don't ..." I muttered, my voice shaky.

"I blame you, too, actually." His eyes were relentless, pinning me to the spot. "You're both accountable for this. To have traveled as much as you have, to have made friends from different cultures, you must have had an open heart and no judgment toward any living creature. But then, you moved into that house. I'm guessing you felt trapped." His gaze was unwavering as he continued, "You probably thought you had to love it all because you loved him. So you made it your number one purpose. And he let you. This"—he motioned to me with a sweep of his hand—"didn't happen overnight."

I stared at him, a tear finally slipping down my cheek, uninvited, unwanted.

"What's *this*?"

"This hardening. Losing yourself."

My mind reeled, my thoughts tumbled over themselves, grasping for clarity, for something solid. Jesse wasn't supposed to be the one giving me this unwanted therapy session. I hadn't asked for this. I hadn't invited him into my head.

I wiped the tear away with the back of my hand. My voice was laced with anger, frustration—vulnerability I didn't want him to see.

"So fucking condescending of you."

"I'm not trying to be." His voice was gentle, his eyes still searching mine. "I'm just being straightforward. Isn't that what you said you wanted? Truth. You said you'd never hate me for telling the truth."

"Truth is subjective." I threw his own words back at him, the ones he'd said to me once.

A pause stretched between us, heavy and loaded with things unsaid. He half-smiled, that infuriating knowing smile, and I felt myself on the edge of something. I didn't want to be having this conversation, but something inside me—something deep—told me I needed to. Even if I didn't like it.

I sighed, not afraid to sound bitter or pissed anymore.

"So, what's your truth? That I'm trying too hard to make them love me?"

His eyes flickered for just a second, but he didn't hesitate.

"That you're waiting for permission."

"Permission?"

"To live your life the way you want. Without worrying about people talking or judging. They don't have that luxury for themselves. But I'm guessing *you* used to. And you're terrified that you'll never feel that free again."

His words hit harder than I expected. My chest tightened, and for a moment, I couldn't breathe.

"Didn't you run away for the same reason? Because you weren't accepted?"

"At first, yeah." There was no tension on his face, just a complete, transparent, overwhelming ... love. But his voice was determined, like he wasn't going to take back any of what he'd said today. "But unlike your travels, which taught you freedom, mine taught me how to be obedient. I learned how to blend in. Cleverly. Without giving up who I was. Today, I blended because I had to. I gave Lazar what he wanted to get what I wanted."

"So, a bargain."

"You could call it that. Or you can call it speaking the right language to a person."

I ignored the linguistic reference he made even though I found it profoundly accurate, but I didn't want to encourage him for choosing the right language with me. Rather, I stuck to my own reference. "And what's your bargain with me?"

He quivered, his expression turning dead-serious.

"I don't bargain with you." He didn't move, his gaze heavy, meaningful. "I'm going all in with you."

A pause. A loaded, heavy pause where I was suddenly acutely aware of every breath, every heartbeat.

"Look," he continued, breaking the silence but not the intensity of the moment, "What I think is you wanted out of that suffocating family situation at first. And when you couldn't get out, you needed proof that you belonged where you ended up. But you couldn't have that either. Because you're different. So I've just given you an out. Take it. But if you care, I can also give you a place to belong. With me."

I stared at him, caught completely off guard. My mouth went dry. The distant sound of a Spider-Man cartoon drifted from the next room, dogs were barking somewhere at the end of the street, a tractor had stopped by the neighbor's house so the driver could chat with a friend, and the birds nesting in the tree outside of the window were engaged in lively conversation.

The world kept spinning, the numbers on the microwave clock ticked forward, and this man I had known for two weeks sat there, looking at me as if his time wouldn't move until I said something.

I managed a choked "Aren't you leaving again?"

"I can stay for something worthwhile." Jesse's voice went husky. "Like the rope park. Or other things that are important." He held my gaze. "I told you, I don't know what you want, Ilaria. So I'm taking it one step at a time. You need to sort this out for yourself. Sell the property or not. Rent if you want. Just move the hell out of that house! You'll still be able to take Milan to see them. You'll still be able to visit Vesna if you want. Just stop smashing your head against the wall."

I felt the weight of his words pressing in on me, suffocating, yet strangely liberating. My mind was a tangled mess, but somewhere in the chaos, there was clarity, which shattered me from the inside just as Jesse added pointedly, "They might not be great, but there are worse people, you know."

I couldn't move, knowing what his next words would be.

"Us." He said matter-of-factly. "We are much worse. For there are so many ways to exist, and we are choosing this one."

What is he saying? That I'm the reason I don't feel at home in my own house? That it's my fault that I expect betrayal from people I should call family? That I'm wrong that I put my child's well-being above everything? That I've endured this for so long just to prove that I can ...?

Sometimes it feels like they're draining the life out of me.

Could he be right? He couldn't possibly be right. He couldn't be building his proposition for a shared future on blame. All this time, every time I'd opened up to him about what was gnawing at me, was he taking notes in his mental journal to hold it later against me like this?

Apparently, I relaxed too easily thinking he was on *my* team.

I took a deep breath, my lungs burning as I inhaled sharply. Clearing my throat, I called for Milan.

"What are you doing?" Jesse asked, his eyes following me as I grabbed my dress and purse, a line formed on his forehead.

"Doing what you told me to. Dealing with it."

"Ilaria—" He stood up.

I cut him off, "You think you're helping me, but you just ..." My voice trembled, teeth clenched against the flood of emotion building inside.

Jesse's eyes darkened. "Ilaria, I'm just trying to—"

"Control me," my chest tightened as I spoke the truth I hadn't wanted to admit. "You think you know what's best for me, and maybe it's coming from a good place, but you're no different from Lazar in this." His jaw twitched at that, but I pressed on. "You're making choices for me, deals behind my back, like I'm incapable of handling things myself."

He moved towards me, but I threw my hand out.

"I can't breathe like this. You've turned this into something about what *you* think I need, but that's not how this works."

He opened his mouth to protest, but I'd already made up my mind. I called Milan again, refusing to let Jesse's quiet hurt sway me.

And when Milan said his goodbyes to Jesse, and Jesse responded quietly, smiling despite himself, "Bye, big guy," it hit me right in the gut. I didn't want to create another cold, impassable gap, and I hated him for making me feel like I don't have to be alone in this, like my son has somebody else in his life who cares about him. I hated him for giving us both this misleading sense of stability that—when it ruptures—would eventually make us fall even harder on our faces, breaking all our teeth out.

No. I will take all the impact myself this time and catch my boy.

I gripped my son's hand as we stepped out of Jesse's house, swallowing my tears again as Milan asked me, "Mom, are we going to come back here later?"

"It's time to go home, baby. It will all be fine again."

11

" DAMN ESPRESSO MACHINE ... How the hell do I—" Petar stormed out of the storeroom with the operation manual in hand, muttering to himself as he brushed past our table and headed straight for the bar. Nina's gaze followed him, glued to his denim-clad buttocks. Her eyes lingered a little too long before flicking back to me with a wicked grin.

"Is he single?"

I glanced at Petar, now squinting furiously between the machine and the manual. "Petar? He dated one of the waitresses here, but judging by his recent tone with her, I'm guessing that ship has sailed."

Nina smirked, a spark of interest lighting her eyes. "Challenge accepted."

I groaned inwardly, rolling my eyes. Classic Nina. I probably looked like hell—at least I felt like it—and it had to be showing on my face because she let out an exaggerated sigh and said, "I get that you're pining—"

I shot her a pointed look.

"—but we just finished unpacking your boxes in that gorgeous new apartment. I was kinda hoping it'd cheer you up. You're off work for another week, you're out of that snake pit, and no one's gonna be poking their nose into your business anymore. All your efforts are paying off. That's worth celebrating, don't you think?"

I leaned back in my chair, staring at the coffee shop ceiling as if it held some hidden wisdom. Nina's words rattled around my brain, but my thoughts kept drifting back to four days ago. The day I had that fight with Jesse, I'd called the owner of the apartment I'd been eyeing for a while. It turned out to still be available, so the next day I packed up and moved. No hesitation, no contemplating. It was as if Jesse gave me the right scissors to cut these ties.

I was still using my time away from him to cool off and give both of us a chance to think things through.

I was giving him an out, and I hoped he knew that.

Go while I'm not looking. I'm too much trouble. I'm not ready. This is too intense.

Danche accidentally spilling water all over my phone the day I left kept me conveniently unreachable. Phoneless, I spent the past few days adjusting to the new location, mapping out new routes, and arranging new spots for Milan's and my things in our cozy little space. No calls, no messages, no distractions—just reflecting on the aftermath.

In the silence of those four days, a painful realization hit me: Jesse was right—I had dragged things out, letting the situation get messier than it needed to be. I could've solved it sooner, avoiding all that drama. I must have let the roots of that family tree tangle around me, making me a part of the house—like Bill Bootstrap Turner.

Another thing I realized during those four days of silence: I missed Jesse like hell. I missed his warm, steady presence, the sound of his voice that made me feel in tune and at peace. His overwhelming affection that swirled around me, and how it made me want to give him all the best parts of myself in return.

Yesterday, when my phone finally came back from the repair shop, I'd tried calling him, only to hear, "out of reach." My stomach dropped. I'd even gone to his house, but no one was home. The sinking feeling grew—had he left again? A new country, a new contract ... Without saying goodbye?

I don't bargain with you. I'm going all in with you.

He did go all in—I felt that. But I must have pushed him away, taking the last reason he had to try harder to embrace the local lifestyle.

But wasn't that exactly what I'd expected from him? He said he could stay here, probably even believed it at the time, but given how many times he'd fled this place, how long could that resolve last?

I'd even tried messaging Betty, just to confirm he was gone. But we weren't friends on Facebook, so my messages went straight into that dark void of requests no one ever checks. Did I even want to know? Did I want him to be gone? Fewer complications, less uncertainty—but no more all-consuming, head-spinning, earth-moving Jesse.

There are worse people, you know. We are much worse. For there are so many ways to exist, and we are choosing this one.

"I'm sorry. I know I'm a mess today," I muttered, shaking off the spiralling thoughts.

Nina raised a perfectly sculpted brow. "Today? Girl, you've been a mess for days. But don't worry, I've got the cure. Cocktails. Followed by reckless decisions. Preferably involving Petar's tight ass."

I cackled, clamping a hand over my mouth as Nina joined in, a mischievous gleam in her eyes.

We were the only customers inside the café, and since it was well past 2 pm, the sliding wall was closed, separating us from the few full tables outside. That meant we could laugh out loud without disturbing anyone's lunch conversation. But I had spotted Vlatko, sipping his beer with two men and a woman on the other side of the glass, so I still had a reason to stay quiet—I wasn't sure I could fake smiles today.

Petar's voice rose in frustration. "The damn machine still won't work. The steam valve's busted or something."

Nina gracefully turned in her chair. "Petar, sweetheart, need help with that espresso machine?"

He looked surprised, his gaze shifting between her and the faulty equipment. "You know about espresso machines?"

Nina stood up, flipping her hair over her shoulder with a smirk. "Honey, I've worked in enough coffee shops to practically be a barista engineer. Let me take a look."

Petar stepped aside, letting Nina behind the counter. She hustled the bartender girl away and crouched to inspect the valve. I lingered near the counter, watching Nina work her magic while Petar gawped at her hands, clearly impressed by the confident precision of her movements. But my attention soon waned, and I headed back to our table—where I almost bumped into Vlatko.

Great. Exactly what I wanted to avoid.

Vlatko's smile spread across his face in that creepy, too-wide way of his, blocking my path with his greasy energy.

"Hey, Ilaria," he said, leaning in a little too close. "You're looking ... good."

I forced a polite smile. "Thanks, Vlatko. Just grabbing a seat."

As I tried to step around him, his arm shot out, casually resting against the wall, as if we were still in the middle of a friendly chat. His smile didn't waver, but there was something darker behind it. My stomach churned. Just then, my eyes flicked toward the café door as it swung open, and my breath caught in my throat.

Jesse.

A familiar set of shoulders under a red T-shirt, his hair a bit shorter than the last time I dug my fingers into it, sunglasses perched on his nose, but even without seeing his eyes, I knew the moment he spotted me. His lips parted slightly, his body stiffened.

He was back. *Was he back?* Had he even been gone in the first place?

"Look, I've been thinking," Vlatko's words dragged my attention back to him. "Last time we talked, you said you weren't interested in dating, but I've heard you're back on the market now."

My stomach twisted. I wondered where he'd heard that from.

Oh, right. Two hundred guests at Sasha's wedding had seen me not-so-casually dancing with a man. The same man now walking toward us, my heart hammering in my chest. Jesse's jaw muscles flexed as he took in the situation, his eyes darting between Vlatko and me.

"So, I was thinking ..." Vlatko went on, reaching for my hand that hung limp at my side, "maybe we could grab dinner? A beer? I live close by."

I started at the unwelcome brush of his fingers against my knuckles.

Just then, Jesse slumped into the chair at the table next to us, making no effort to hide his irritation. Taking off his sunglasses, he looked directly at me, completely ignoring Vlatko.

"So, I feel like I overstepped last time," Jesse's voice was cold, sharp, "and I should ask: do you want me to interfere now? Because this dickhead is clearly asking for it."

The space between him and Vlatko suddenly felt suffocating. Vlatko's thick brows knitted as he stared at Jesse, who was calm—but in that dangerous, simmering way that suggested he could explode at any second.

Full-throttle Jesse.

I shot him a nonchalant look, trying to keep my voice steady. "I can handle it."

Turning to Vlatko, I straightened. "I really appreciate the offer, but I'm not back on the market."

I hoped my voice sounded final, though my hands shook, and the skin Vlatko had touched still prickled unpleasantly. I could feel Jesse's eyes on me, and when I glanced at him, the question in my gaze was clear: *Happy now?*

Vlatko looked at me like he was catching at a straw, his lips twitched into a nervous smile. "Does that mean ...?"

Jesse's voice sliced through the air. "It means you can be excused, Inspector."

An unfathomable exchange passed between them in the next ten seconds, like they made their points without words. But the way Jesse said "Inspector"—so specific, so pointed—I knew he'd looked him up after what I'd told him. Jesse knew people. That's what that tone and unflinching stare meant.

Vlatko muttered something under his breath before walking

away, and I finally exhaled the breath I hadn't realized I'd been holding.

Jesse leaned back in his chair, his gaze softening just slightly. "You alright there?"

I took a moment, steadying my breath. I didn't want him to see me like this, but it was too late. Jesse's brows furrowed. "Ilaria. Are you okay?"

I wasn't okay. And Vlatko was only half the reason.

I sat down across from Jesse. It wasn't even my table, but Nina wouldn't mind as she was still tinkering with the espresso machine behind the bar, completely oblivious to the tension hanging between us.

I studied him, he looked ruffled: there was a rough stubble on his sharp jawline and chin, and tired shadows under his eyes.

"Weren't you supposed to have left?" I asked.

Jesse's eyes searching mine. "I did leave. But I came back this morning."

"Why?"

He narrowed his eyes at me, confusion flashing across his face. "What do you mean, *why*? I live here."

"But I thought ... Your phone was off, your gate was locked from the outside, and Petar said you'd left," I said, feeling the ache rise in my throat.

Jesse's brow furrowed. "*Your* phone was off! I tried calling you the next morning."

"That was a water-spilling accident," I muttered. "I just got my phone back from the repair shop yesterday."

"I thought you switched it off, and I went by your place."

"What? When?" My pulse quickened at the thought that I might've missed him.

"Two days ago, before I flew out. Lazar told me you moved out and didn't say where. I had zero idea on how to look for you!"

"Wait, if you weren't leaving for good, where have you been?" I asked, struggling to make sense of everything, the knots in my chest tightening with each word.

"Leaving for good? Ilaria, I went to Turkey to meet a prospect. You thought I'd left for good?"

"Petar said you flew out, so I assumed ..." I trailed off.

"Petar!" Jesse called, his voice sharp. Petar's chestnut head popped up from behind the bar, startled.

"Oh, you're here," Petar stammered. "I'm almost done with my shift. Just fixing this damn coffee maker, and I'll be right with you."

From behind the bar, over the high-pitched hiss of steam, Nina's voice chimed in, "Call it 'coffee maker' one more time, and it'll start adding milk to your Americano."

Jesse turned his head back to Petar, unimpressed. "Why didn't you tell Ilaria I was only gone for a day?"

Petar squinted at Jesse, confusion written all over his face, and Nina appeared beside him, clearly intrigued by the drama unfolding. Petar's gaze bounced between the two of us, probably thinking why Jesse thought I was entitled to know about his whereabouts. "Did I ... miss something here?"

Nina clapped him on the shoulder with condescension. "Oh, you have no idea, buddy."

Jesse exhaled sharply, pinching the bridge of his nose. "You thought I left? Ilaria ..." His voice dropped, low and sincere, filled with regret. "I made a mistake. I shouldn't have pushed you or schemed behind your back. You were right. But when I said I'd stay, I meant it. I'm not changing my mind."

My vision blurred, tears gathered in my eyes too quickly, I couldn't possibly be one step ahead to blink them away.

Jesse's gaze softened further when he saw me breaking down. He reached across the table, his rough, warm fingers curling gently around my trembling hand. His thumb traced slow circles on my skin, a gesture so simple, but it felt like he was offering me an anchor in the chaos.

I was so wrong. He was not the one bringing complications and uncertainty into my life. He was all the opposite things.

"You thought I'd just leave you?" His voice was barely above a whisper, but the emotion in it cut right through me. His eyes, intense and searching, locked onto mine as if he could see every wall I'd built up crumbling before him.

A loud metallic clank echoed through the café, followed by a triumphant sound from Nina and Petar. "Yes!" Petar yelled, fist-pumping the air. "She fixed it! No more espresso disasters!"

Nina's delighted laugh followed as she patted Petar on the back, and he walked out from behind the counter, phone and wallet in hand. "Alright, I'm done. Let's go," he said to Jesse, oblivious to the moment he'd just interrupted.

Jesse glanced at Petar, like he'd just remembered something, but his hand stayed firmly in mine. "Sorry, man, give me a minute."

Petar looked at our hands on the table and groaned, rolling his eyes dramatically. "Man, does this mean I'm going to have to watch football by myself?"

Nina grabbed her purse and hooked her arm through Petar's, squeezing my upper arm as she passed. "I love football. Where? The Green Pub?"

Petar startled, assessing her fabulous grin. "Uh ... yeah, the Green Pub."

"Perfect," Nina said, dragging him toward the exit. She shot me a wink over her shoulder before disappearing out the door with Petar in tow.

As the door closed behind them, the café fell into a gentle hum, with the distant sound of traffic and the quiet clinking of dishes from the kitchen. The waiter who had taken over Petar's shift darted between the counter and the outdoor tables, balancing bottles of Schweppes, beers, and cups of macchiato. I slipped my hand from Jesse's grip to brush the wet off my cheeks and push the loose strands of hair off my face.

"So, you went to Turkey, huh?" I asked, suddenly realised I didn't even remember what my hair looked like and what I had managed to throw on before leaving the apartment. But I also realised I didn't care.

"Yeah. Had a business dinner and flew back with a night flight."

"Did you get the client?"

"Pretty sure I did," he said with an even dull tone.

I tried to fit enough excitement into my voice for both of us, "That's great news, Jesse!"

He pressed his lips together to a faint smile, and then asked. "What did you say happened to your phone?"

"Danche spilled water on it while helping me move the boxes."

"She was *helping* you?" There was something incredulous in his tone.

"Yeah. Just like you said, she's very friendly now." I let out a small, humorless laugh. The kind that never quite reaches your eyes.

Jesse's brows pulled together. "Does that mean everything is good between you?"

I shrugged, my fingers nervously tracing the edge of the wooden menu stand. "I think it is ... or it can be, if I keep her at a distance. She even bought me a new phone that day—immediately."

"She did?"

I nodded slowly, glancing at the table where Nina and I had been sitting earlier. "Yeah, but ... it's still in the box. I didn't want it. That one ..." I pointed at the phone on the table, "Stefan bought it for me, and I couldn't give it up. There are so many photos I never managed to transfer. The minute that screen went black, I thought I'd lost all of them."

To be honest, that moment had felt like the greatest tragedy and the greatest liberation at the same time. That had been when I'd seen everything clearly, as if I had stepped out of my body and looked at all that mess from the outside.

I looked up at Jesse, searching his eyes for permission to go on with an uncomfortable confession. "To be honest, I think I wasn't moving out because of *him*. I felt like I had to stay, to protect his things, his interests. On his behalf." I shook my head. "It's so stupid."

Jesse leaned back, his gaze softening as he took in my words. "It's not stupid. You had every reason to feel that way. They've done everything to make you believe they'd discard whatever Stefan left behind."

We held each other's gaze in silence, and my throat felt like sandpaper. I'd been fooling myself into thinking I'd be better off without him, without this extraordinary man who never once made me feel like a foreigner around him.

Breaking the stillness, Jesse asked as he looked at the play area, "Where's Milan?"

"With Vesna. I dropped him off an hour ago."

"So ... Where did you move to?"

"An apartment across from the Archaeological Museum."

Jesse nodded thoughtfully, but I wasn't done with admissions.

"You were right. I got stuck there, in that house. You tried to help me see that, and I ... I was a massive bitch—again."

Jesse shook his head, leaning forward again. "No, you weren't. I overreacted. I just ... freaked out."

"Freaked out?"

He let out a heavy breath, rubbing the back of his neck, looking vulnerable. "Last time, in my previous relationship ... I left things hanging. I thought she'd work it out with her family, but everything fell apart. Looking back, I know I could have fought for it more. And then, seeing you stuck in that situation with your in-laws ... it felt like déjà vu. I thought if it didn't settle, you'd slip away too. And that terrified the shit out of me. So I overstepped. I was acting out of fear."

His raw honesty was bone-crushing. I lowered my gaze, tracing the engraved "Tuscany Café" on the menu holder with my finger. "I'm sorry, Jesse. I know I'm a lot to handle, and I never wanted you to feel like you had to solve my problems."

Jesse's hand slid across the table, palm up, waiting for mine. When I placed my hand in his, the warmth soothed my hyped nerves like sorcery. "But I *want* this, Ilaria. I want *you* to be real with me, and if you have problems, I want to be the one you come to. I want you in my bed, I want your rants and your history lessons. And if you get tired of that apartment—and I suspect you will, because let's be honest, you need a yard for your morning coffee—then I want you to move in with me. My house is big and empty, and no one has ever lived in it properly. That house is meant for family, Ilaria. And I want you to furnish it however you like. I want Milan to bring all his cars, scatter them everywhere, disassemble them, and I'll put them all back together."

I stared at him, my heart pounding as he continued, his words pouring out with a fierce intensity that left me breathless. "I want us to go public. Because if some dipshit like Vlatko Bozhenov—or anyone else—ever assumes you're 'back on the market' again, I swear, I'll lose it."

A lump rose in my throat. His words weren't just promises; they were declarations—bold, unyielding. I could hardly find my voice. "Jesse ..."

He put his second hand on top of our intertwined fingers, his voice softening. "And if it's too fast, we'll take it slow. I don't mind. If you want to give this thing a shot and don't want to rush into the big, serious picture I've painted, that's fine. We'll move at your pace. I'll never pressure you again."

I swallowed, fighting back the tears welling in my eyes. "Are you really staying?"

Jesse's lips curved into a small smile, his thumb brushing over my knuckles. "I sold the vineyards. I'm already looking for a venue for the rope park. I'm staying, Ilaria."

"But you said you need a change of scenery occasionally. What will happen when you get sick and tired of this place?"

"I said *we both* need a change of scenery occasionally. We'll travel. Whenever we need to. People invented cars and planes for a reason."

A quiet laugh escaped my throat as I wiped a tear from the corner of my eye. "I hope you don't mind public displays of affection, because I plan on kissing you whenever I want— whether it's in the middle of a parking lot, a supermarket, or a beach. If I'm doing this, I want all of it."

His grin widened as he stood up and walked over to me, pulling me gently to my feet. And it all came rushing back to me: the intoxicating feeling of his firm warm body against mine, the smell of his skin that liquified my bones, the contagious darkness of his irises that fastened my heartbeat by the second. His hands gripped my waist, his voice low and teasing. "You can PDA the hell out of me, Ilaria."

And then he kissed me. Everything I had missed for the last four days flooded back in that moment, like a force too strong to contain. I knew we had an audience—people were probably watching through the glass—some giving us side-long glances, while others were less subtle, staring and smirking.

But they had a right to judge, just as I had a right to ignore them. Because among so many things in my life that had been forced, stretched, and twisted, this felt instinctive—like a second skin. It made me believe, almost religiously, that we were meant to meet like this—by some tangled plan, in the middle of chaos—just to make each other feel like we belong. With nothing but the grip of our hands and a shared, reckless, 'why the hell not?'

Two foreigners. On the same team.

Epilogue

Three years later

THE SUN SHIMMERED off the lake's surface, casting a dazzling mosaic of light across the water. From where I sat on the wooden deck Jesse had built, the world felt almost unreal in its beauty—like a painting brought to life. My legs dangled over the edge, submerged in the pleasantly cool water that rippled gently against my skin. Green hills surrounded the bay, their soft slopes protecting me from the screeching heat that had already begun its reign over Ohrid this time of year in July. Here, though, in this little oasis, everything felt perfectly balanced. The air, the water, the earth—it all felt like home.

Jesse had built this house for me on the land I bought by the lake. It started as a weekend getaway, but now it was so much more. He'd worked on every detail himself, like it was his own personal gift to me. And in a way, it was—his love made real through bricks and beams, nails and wood. Our retreat, our refuge from the world. I looked out at the boat floating near the deck. I'd only bought it a few days ago. It still needed a fresh coat of paint, and we hadn't decided on a name yet, but it was ours. A little piece of freedom, waiting to take us wherever we wanted.

My phone buzzed, breaking the stillness. I glanced down at the screen and smiled. A notification from Dino Space. I opened it to see a new photo: a dozen 10-year-olds in paintball gear, their faces lit with excitement. Jesse, Nina, and Petar were posing with them, all three wearing the Dino Space staff T-shirts. I chuckled. They looked like they were having the time of their lives.

Jesse and I had been running Dino Space for two years now—birthday parties, kids' get-togethers, all managed by Nina with Petar helping out between shifts at *Tuscany*. The business had blossomed, and now, with their wedding coming up in September, Jesse and I would have to find someone to cover for them during their honeymoon.

The photo must have been taken yesterday and only posted now. I could have been in it too if I wasn't here, tucked away by the lake. Jesse had brought me to Ohrid a week ago, insisting I focus on my final exams at the Faculty of Tourism and Hospitality. I'd passed the first one—two more to go. And while I was here, Jesse had taken over everything back home, juggling Dino Space, Milan, and life in between. Vesna had been more than eager to take Milan whenever Jesse needed help. She constantly insisted on my husband coming for dinner, always bragging to everyone, saying, *"My girl is in such good hands."* Now he was part of her resume, too.

My phone rang, and Jesse's voice crackled through the speaker, loud against the sound of wind rushing through his open window.

"Is the water cold?" he asked, his tone playful.

"The water is perfect," I said, smiling into the phone. "Come and swim with me."

"We're on the way," he said, and then I heard Milan's excited voice in the background.

"Hey, Mom! We're bringing the tools—we'll be fixing the eaves!"

"Great news!" I laughed. "You know I love watching my boys work—just as long as I'm not asked to help."

Jesse's chuckle was warm and familiar. "Once I get there, you can put your feet up and read all day."

"No board games?" I teased.

"I'm bringing three new ones," he replied. "So ... "

"Oh, perfect! Another opportunity to absolutely destroy you all."

"Big talk," Jesse shot back, "for someone who gets stuck in Uno loops."

I gasp dramatically.

"Vesna sent a container of sarma with me for you."

"Of course she did!" I roll my eyes, making a mental note to call my former mother-in-law.

"Hey, I've been thinking," Jesse said, his voice turning thoughtful. "How about Veronica?"

I looked at the boat that rocked gently in place, white paint clinging to the wood in uneven patches. "Babe, I told you—it doesn't have to be your mom's name or my mom's. It doesn't have to be anybody's grandma either."

"I know," he laughed. "But I kinda like Veronica."

"You'll decide when you see her," I said, grinning.

"Okay, okay," he conceded. "I'm stopping to grab a coffee, then we're hitting the highway. See you in a couple of hours."

"Drive safe."

I set the phone down, resting it carefully away from the water's edge. This deck could use a railing, I think. Baby Veronica—if that's who she'll be—will need something to hold onto when she starts coming here, toddling her first summer steps beside me. My hand instinctively finds my rounded belly, stroking lightly as if asking for her opinion. *Does Veronica feel right?*

I pause, waiting for some unspoken sign, but the truth is, I know better. Like Milan, we will have to meet her first, see her face, feel her presence, before her name will truly reveal itself. The boat, bobbing by the dock, will remain nameless a little longer. A couple more months.

I sit there for a moment, feeling the transparent water inviting me in. The same water that used to unnerve me, that vast, endless unknown stretching beneath the surface like a void waiting to swallow me whole. I once thought I'd disappear in it, dissolve into its depths without a trace, without the strength to come back up for air.

But now, as I slide off the deck and let my body dip into the lake's embrace, I'm not afraid. The water no longer frightens me—it holds me.

And I just swim.

ABOUT THE AUTHOR

Irina Angelova has moved between countries her entire life, to the point where she's not sure where home really is. Pieces of her heart belong to Japan, Malta, China, India, and Macedonia. Currently, Irina lives in North Macedonia, raising her two children and two dogs, and loving her husband, while working as a pedagogical designer and content creator. This work gives her the freedom to write whenever and wherever she wants—often, like a true writer, in a coffee shop with her laptop in hand.